THE GLAD EYE

Also by Stan Barstow

THE
GLAD EYE
and other stories

STAN BARSTOW

MICHAEL JOSEPH
LONDON

First published in Great Britain by Michael Joseph Ltd
44 Bedford Square, London WC1
1984

Acknowledgments for those stories first published
elsewhere are made to the editors of *Dandelion
Clocks*, *Loving Couples*, *Winter's Tales 28*, *Woman* and
Woman's Own

British Library Cataloguing in Publication Data

Barstow, Stan
The glad eye.
I. Title
823'.914[F]   PR6052.A75
ISBN 0 7181 2440 5

Photoset by Rowland Phototypesetting Ltd, Suffolk
Printed and bound in Great Britain by
Billings and Sons Ltd, Worcester.

To Sid and René Chaplin

Contents

Work in Progress

Otterburn had come to live in this cathedral city when he left his wife. He rented a room and kitchen, with a shared bath and lavatory on the next landing. He had never lived alone in his life before and from his window he could look down three floors at the river flowing between its stone banks and think that at least he hadn't far to go if he decided to do away with himself.

The river ran through the city under four bridges. Upstream was the bishop's palace, which Otterburn had not yet seen. The city was a great tourist attraction and at every season of the year, though more plentiful in summer, damp crocodiles of children and groups of visitors speaking many different languages could be found in the narrow streets and around the cathedral, whose walls of pale carved stone were just now free of masons' scaffolding for the first time in years. It sometimes seemed to Otterburn that every corner one turned gave fresh evidence of the city's beauty. He soon found also, as others who had come to live here before him had discovered, that the damp air gave him recurring trouble with his sinuses.

One day, coming into the house, he found an envelope addressed to him on the mat behind the door. It surprised him, for no one knew he was here. Yet this was an envelope with his name written on it in someone's hand. He took it upstairs and opened it in his room. There was a single sheet of rather good dove-grey writing-paper, folded once. On it, written in the same hand, was the message: 'I shall be in the Ferryboat at seven tonight.' Nothing more. No signature. No date. Otterburn could not decide whether it was a woman's handwriting or a man's. He looked at the envelope again. There was no stamp or postmark. It had presumably been delivered by its sender. And seven tonight meant just that.

The Ferryboat was a riverside pub a couple of minutes' walk away, a smart place with a colourful inn sign and well-kept white paint on the outside. Its rooms were small but cosy and always spotlessly clean. Its brass and mirrors gleamed. On cooler days wood fires burned in the grates. Small dishes of olives and tiny silver onions and potato crisps stood on the bar counter in the lounge. At one end of the counter at lunchtime joints of cold ham and roast beef rested on a white cloth and cuts of these were offered with jacket potatoes and a green salad or as the filling between slices of crusty bread. On warm days then, and sometimes on balmy evenings, the clientele would spill out on to the embankment, to drink at tables on the cobbles and watch perhaps a skiff with a lone rower speed upstream or a white pleasure boat glide by.

The Ferryboat was Otterburn's local but he had been in only a couple of times. Its food was expensive and its drinks always a few pence dearer than in the other pubs nearby, and Otterburn was being careful with his money. Otterburn's wife would not want, because her father had money. It was only when he had won a prize in a premium-bond draw that Otterburn had finally decided to break away from his wife. His windfall had been twenty thousand pounds. His idea was to live on it until he sorted himself out; but inflation would cut into its value, and with over three million unemployed the prospects of finding another job were not good. Not that Otterburn relished the thought of working for someone else again, but he would have to earn a living in some way when the money ran out. Unless he did do away with himself. There had been times when that had seemed the only way of freeing himself from Hazel. He had thought also of leaving her, but until his good fortune he had had no money.

Otterburn also had a daughter, but as she was a pupil at a boarding school he saw her only during the holidays. The combined influence of Otterburn's wife and the school had given the girl a distant manner and sometimes she would treat Otterburn as though she was not quite sure who he was and wondered why he should be there every time she came home.

She had certainly always been made aware that it was her grandfather's money that, directly or indirectly, kept everything going. When Otterburn had finally fallen to wondering why Hazel had married him in the first place, he reached the reluctant conclusion that it satisfied something in her nature to be able to choose a potential failure, confirm him in that role and dominate him because of it. 'Thee stick by thi family an' thi job, Malcolm lad,' Otterburn's father-in-law had said to him early on, 'an' tha'll never want for owt. Is'll see to that.' That the rich little business in importing and exporting specialised foodstuffs that Hazel's father had created and built up could carry one passenger was the interpretation Otterburn came to put on the situation. 'Sufferance,' he had finally said to himself. 'That's what I'm living on. Sufferance.'

Otterburn looked again at the note. He thought on reflection that the writing was more probably a woman's than a man's. Then again, it had almost a childish look. If that were so, he told himself, it was not because it belonged to a young person but because its backward slope was a disguise.

He heated chicken soup for his lunch, the remains of the can he had opened yesterday. Otterburn had not been able to cook when he came to the house, beyond boil and fry eggs and grill bacon. Now he could scramble eggs and soon he would master the making of omelettes. He was determined, with the help of a basic cookbook, to learn how to feed himself on a simple but balanced diet. At present he fell back more often than he liked on expensive frozen foods, but he intended before long to be knowledgeable in buying the ingredients for casseroles and stews, the buying and preparation of his own fish and in making pancakes and vegetarian dishes which would cut his intake of meat. In the meantime he heated the soup and cut bread and thought about what he might have for his evening meal which would fit in with his visit to the Ferryboat at seven.

But who said he was going to the Ferryboat? Why in heaven should he take the slightest notice of a message from someone who couldn't sign his or her name?

Because it showed that someone was interested in him.

After he'd eaten, and drunk two cups of tea, Otterburn lay down on his bed which, with a woven cover over it, doubled as a divan. He had not done anything physically strenuous but he felt tired. He felt tired rather a lot lately. With no routine to shape and control his day, indolence took over. He should, he thought, make some kind of plan for occupying his time. Perhaps he might study in depth the history of the city, embarking on a programme of reading with the aid of the public library. With nothing to distract him, he could become an expert. From the trunk of the subject he could explore the many branches, political and economic, religious and secular. Perhaps he could eventually write some articles himself and publish them under a pseudonym. Or even a book.

Mildly excited by the prospect, Otterburn dozed off.

He woke to find himself wondering what he should wear this evening. He'd been accustomed to sports jackets and jumpers and slacks, and off-the-peg business suits of un-memorable cut and cloth. His shirts were in plain white or pastel shades, or with faint stripes on a white ground. He almost always wore a tie, feeling undressed without one unless he had on a sweater whose neck came up about his throat. He had no style. A lot of men who frequented the Ferryboat had style, even if it was only in the careless way they wore a T-shirt with patched and faded jeans. Otterburn did not want to go to that extreme. It only worked if you felt not the slightest trace of self-consciousness. But there was room for some improvement.

He looked at his watch. It was only the middle of the afternoon. There was still time for him to catch the bank open. Otterburn had stopped using his credit card for fear that when he informed the company of his change of address his wife would trace him. His prize from the premium bond he had kept secret from her. Somehow he had realised immediately the opportunity it gave him, so he had said nothing and deposited the money in an account at a new bank, transferring it yet again when he moved to this city.

Leaving the house, Otterburn walked briskly along the quay and up a sloping alley to emerge into the street. There were several men's outfitters of quality, some specialising in shirts and knitwear, some in suits of clothes, others in shoes; and a couple of department stores who could equip one from head to foot and from the skin out. He stopped as he passed the windows of one such and thought that he could go in and pay by cheque when he knew what his outlay was. But then, he might this evening find himself called upon to stand drinks, or even a meal, and it would be as well to have spare cash in his pocket. So he walked to the bank, made a withdrawal with three minutes to spare, then retraced his steps.

In the store he selected a two-piece casual suit in blue denim and took it into a cubicle. One thing, he thought as he appraised himself in the glass, was that though he was no longer a lad he still had a lean body that didn't need forcing into slim-hipped trousers. The cubicle mirrors gave him views of his profile and the back of his head. His first thought was that he needed a haircut, his second that he didn't. His hair at this stage in its growth waved quite becomingly in the nape of his neck. If left for another couple of weeks it would be long enough for a restyling by a barber who knew more than the short-back-and-sides Otterburn had always favoured, simply from long habit. Perhaps he could brush it forward instead of back and dispense with that neat parting he had fought so long to establish when a boy. From this, Otterburn went on to the question of his spectacles. He didn't think he needed to indulge in the vanity of contact lenses: the appearance of many men was enhanced by their glasses. What he should try was a more modern type of frame, with larger lenses. But these were longer-term considerations. For the present he felt and looked well in the denim suit. The effect would be complemented when he added a new shirt. He chose one of wide navy-blue and narrow pale-pink stripes, with a scarlet thread running through the pink, then paid for his purchases with cash. The suit he thought quite cheap, though the shirt cost more than he was used to paying. He left with the goods in a large carrier bag with the name of the store printed on it and walked back to his room through the warm and slightly hazy air of the afternoon.

Taking advantage of the quietness of the house, Otterburn went down and ran a hot bath. He lay in it for some time, watching, his thoughts in the same suspended state, his pubic hair and his limp penis float under the surface of the water. Otterburn rarely indulged in sexual reverie. Though his intimate life with Hazel had consisted of an efficient but matter-of-fact once-a-week Saturday-night coupling, a routine relief usually initiated by her and never referred to out of the bed, it had been enough to keep him from fancying women on the street and from longing for some more intense liaison. He supposed he was undersexed. He thought, on the occasions when it crossed his mind, that he was lucky. It had seemed enough for Hazel and its absence had not preoccupied him since he had left her. Now he wondered if the letter was not drawing him to the beginning of a sexual adventure. The letter . . . He could still hardly believe it was real and he had opened it and read it again before coming down for his bath. The distant nudging of common sense told him he was being foolish in taking so much trouble to prepare for an assignation made in such a mysterious fashion. But it *was* distant. His mind was as languorous as his body, drifting, floating, waiting for whatever might happen.

Someone was interested in him . . .

The skin of his fingertips was wrinkled. He had not known that since he had played in his bath as a child. He pulled the plug and stood up, putting a quick steadying hand to the wall as a faint giddiness made his head spin. He had stayed in too long. He took his sponge and squeezed water from the cold tap over himself.

Back in his room, he pulled on pyjama trousers under his dressing-gown and tucked a scarf round his neck. The squeaking groan of an unoiled pulley drew him to the window. Some men were unloading bales into a warehouse from a barge across the river. Otterburn dragged a chair over and sat down to watch.

On his way to the Ferryboat, Otterburn strolled up the alley to the street and bought an evening paper. It would give him a prop with which to occupy his eyes and hands, should he have to wait. How would the approach be made? Would someone simply walk up to him, smile and say, 'Did you get my letter?' It was at this point that he wondered if he were about to be faced with some wrongdoing from his past. We could all, he told himself, feel the occasional touch of a nameless anxiety: that was a part of the human condition. Yet, as he cast his mind back over the dull march of his years, he could find no specific

act of his that merited guilt. He had lived a blameless life. His
trouble was that he could not imagine anyone's being interested in him for his own sake.

He had decided that it would be better if he were a few
minutes early; he could watch then who came into the pub, and
it would save him from feeling that he himself was being
observed as he entered. The pub was at the ebb of its evening
trade. The after-office drinkers were already gone or about to
leave. There were some tourists, who would not linger. The
late evening customers had not yet appeared. Otterburn chose
the lounge. He bought half a pint of bitter, and as two
businessmen left a corner table he went over to it and sat down
with his back to the wall. From here he could see the door at the
far end of the room as well as that at this end of the bar, through
which he had entered. Yes, he must be first, for by no stretch of
the imagination could he picture any of those present as the
author of the note. That group in anoraks were visitors, come
to look at the sights. They in their turn, as they suddenly all
laughed, were being given a quick once-over by the landlord
who, in check Viyella shirt and yellow tie, his glasses hanging
from a cord round his neck, had just come in to join the girl
behind the bar. That elderly gent sitting alone, neat grey hair,
well-cut navy-blue blazer, reading the *Financial Times* and
drinking from a half-pint pewter tankard, lived in that big
bay-windowed house farther along the embankment. And
that middle-aged man and the much younger woman were too
absorbed in each other even to have noticed him except as
someone they needn't fear. An office romance, if he'd ever
seen one. Soon they would go their separate ways, he to make
his excuses at home, she to fill in her time somehow till the
next snatched hour. The only remote possibility was the thin
woman of indeterminate age, in tweeds, sitting at the bar,
lighting a fresh cigarette within seconds of stubbing out the
last, and ordering another gin and tonic, lemon but no ice. But
Otterburn had seen her before too, and if she had wanted to
know him she would have hailed him and drawn him into her
company with the unselfconscious ease with which she chatted
to the barmaid and the landlord and whoever of the regulars
stayed long enough at the bar. You could find her counterpart,
Otterburn reflected, in pubs and hotel bars all over the coun-

try: women who gave the impression of having seen it all, who had settled for a secure but boring marriage to a dull but tolerant husband, to whom they would return each mid-evening, ever so slightly tipsy, after a couple of hours' steady drinking.

In any gathering Otterburn merged with the background, but he prided himself on missing little. He observed and speculated and remained uninvolved. It occurred to him now that this was probably the ideal make-up of a writer. Except that he couldn't write. But how did he know that? There he went, dismissing himself before he had even tried. Wasn't that something else he might explore in his new-found freedom? Of course, while he might be good at noting people's appearance and mannerisms, his speculations about their character and their private lives could be wildly wrong. But did that matter? His guess was that, while a writer might use real people as starting-points, he very soon found himself casting their personalities into the mould of his own. And there *was* an obvious snag. Had he himself enough personality, did he care enough, to be able to draw characters who could make a reader care? Yet Otterburn felt excitement stir again at this second new prospect. He could do no more than try. It amused him, gave him even a strange feeling of power, to think of himself going about noting people not simply from a habit of his nature, but as a collector. If he couldn't think of plots all at once, he could at least keep a written sketchbook and train himself after each outing to record, as objectively as a painter or a photographer, what he had seen and heard.

Otterburn had lifted his newspaper and was looking past it with renewed interest at his fellow drinkers when he saw his wife coming into the room. Intensely startled, he raised the paper higher until his head and shoulders were hidden as Hazel glanced round the room then half-turned to speak to the man who was following her.

There was nowhere for Otterburn to hide. If he got up now, it was unlikely that he could reach the door before she turned again and saw him. But what was she doing here and who was that she was with? From his first startled glance Otterburn couldn't recall ever having seen him before, though he supposed he could have met him and forgotten. In which case the man might remember him, especially if there was something irregular going on.

Otterburn risked moving his paper slightly to one side. His wife had taken a seat at a table in the middle of the floor and now had her back directly to him, showing him a quarter-profile as she removed her gloves and spoke to her companion, who was ordering drinks at the bar. Hazel was looking particularly smart. She had on her best black suit and a white blouse with a jabot, black nylon tights and high-heeled black patent-leather shoes. Her hair was newly washed and set and she had had that blonde rinse which restored its fading colour. He supposed she was, to some eyes, a handsome woman. It was amazing the improvement brought to her legs by the right shoes and stockings. Her hips and her breasts were ample but still shapely, only hinting yet at the excess another few years might bestow. To his surprise, Otterburn felt his flesh stir; as though he didn't know all too well the briskness and lack of finesse with which she despatched sexual appetite. Not that he had had any direct experience to compare that with, but he did read, and today's explicit novels left him in little doubt that there were prolonged delights to which they were both strangers.

In his contemplation of his wife's back, Otterburn had, he suddenly realised, let the paper down until his face was completely visible. And at that moment the man Hazel was with turned with the drinks and looked directly at him. His stare hardened. Otterburn lifted the paper again. After a moment's consternation, he felt himself grinning broadly. Of course the man didn't know him. Otterburn had just been given warning that he was not to ogle his own wife! How rich! Whether or not Hazel and her companion were any more than just good friends, the man was obviously jealous and possessive. What a joke, Otterburn thought, if he were to stare at Hazel until the man felt forced to do something about it. How their faces would fall when Otterburn then went over and let Hazel see him. A pity it wasn't worth it. But it wasn't. Once Hazel knew where he was, she would give him no peace.

She was looking over her shoulder as she picked up her handbag. Her companion nodded to a sign on the wall. She got up and crossed the room without looking at anyone and went out through the door nearest to Otterburn. Otterburn knew where the Ladies was. He gave her a moment to find it herself, then stood up and emptied his glass. The man was staring again. Surprised at his own boldness, Otterburn grinned at him and winked before walking out through the same door.

There was a huge pale American Ford parked on the cobbles outside. For some reason it reminded Otterburn of an enormous double bed. He knew instinctively that it belonged to Hazel's companion. Ownership of such an opulent and extravagant car, parked where no one was supposed to park, fitted exactly that arrogant stare and that black moustache, so thick and neatly trimmed it looked like something glued to the fellow's upper lip. So, Otterburn asked himself, *was* Hazel having an affair, and if so was it one which had started since he left her, or had it been going on before? Further, did it help or hinder him in his new way of life? More to the immediate point was that Hazel's appearance had ruined his own assignation. And what could he do now except wait for them to leave? And by that time might it not be too late?

Otterburn strolled aimlessly along the embankment, tapping the rolled newspaper against his leg. He felt now like someone who has turned up to a party on the wrong night: to a party, in fact, that was already over. 'All dressed up and nowhere to go.' He turned up off the riverside and into the town. A few minutes' aimless walking found him outside the painted window of a pizza parlour. He looked at the menu. He was peckish. He went in. He always maintained that he didn't care for pizzas, but now he wanted something simple and cheap which would satisfy his sudden appetite, if not delight his palate. He ordered at random from the ten or more variations on the menu and asked for a half-pint of lager. The place was busy. There were even some families with quite young children. People were coming and going all the time and the waitresses in their green aprons and matching caps hurried between kitchen and tables without a moment to catch their breath. A young woman came in, stood looking round for a moment, saw that she hadn't much choice, then sat down at the next table. She took a small square of handkerchief from her shoulder bag and polished her glasses before reading the menu. Otterburn read his paper. His pizza came. It was enormous. He picked up his knife and fork, hardly knowing where to make the first incision. He cut a piece. The topping was still sizzling and he gasped, reaching for his lager, as it scorched his mouth. The outer door opened and shut again. A group crowded in.

'D'you mind?' a voice asked.

Otterburn looked up. The girl from the next table had half pulled out the chair opposite him. He didn't understand at first but with a mouthful of pizza he couldn't yet swallow he made noises and waved his knife about. She sat down.

'If I sit here, they can all sit together,' the girl explained. Otterburn looked past her. Five young people had taken possession of the table she had left. He swallowed.

'Very thoughtful of you.'

'It's so very busy tonight.'

'Is that exceptional?'

'Well, no. They seem to do well most nights.'

'You've been in before, then?'

'Yes. It's simple and convenient, and not expensive.'

'Quite. That's what I thought.'

'What is that you've got, if you don't mind my asking?'

Otterburn turned the menu round. 'Er . . . it's a number eleven.'

'It looks good.'

'I'm not an expert on pizzas,' Otterburn said, 'but there's plenty of it and it's very hot.' He swallowed another mouthful. 'And quite tasty too.'

'Mmm.'

A waitress came and put a plate of spaghetti bolognese in front of the girl, then sprinkled grated cheese over it with careless haste. The girl put her fork vertically into the spaghetti, twirled it and lifted some to her mouth. Her light brown hair fell softly across each cheek as she bent her head slightly forward.

'You've done that before,' Otterburn said.

'Yes. I lived in Italy for a while. The only reason I eat this after what I got used to there is because it's cheap.'

'It's not a country I know,' Otterburn said. 'I've been to Spain, but not Italy.'

'Do you live here?' the girl asked.

'Yes. Do you?'

'I do just now, yes.'

'What's your job?'

'Oh, I'm sort of in-between things.'

'I suppose a lot of people are like that just now.'

'Yes. What do you do?' Otterburn hesitated. The girl said, 'I'm sorry, if you don't want to tell me. But you did ask *me*.'

'I'm a writer, actually,' Otterburn said.

'Oh? That must be interesting. Would I have heard of you? Do you write under your own name or a pseudonym?'

'You won't have heard of me,' Otterburn said. 'My name's Otterburn. Malcolm Otterburn.'

The girl was frowning politely. 'No, I'm afraid I haven't. And it's quite an unusual name, isn't it? I mean, not one you'd forget.'

'Think nothing of it,' Otterburn said.

'I can see now why you hesitated to tell me, though,' the girl said. 'It must be terribly embarrassing to say you're a writer and people have never heard of you.'

'It happens all the time,' Otterburn said. 'But you haven't told me your name.'

Now it was her turn to appear reluctant. 'Promise me you won't laugh.'

'Why on earth should I laugh?'

'Because this is where *I* always get embarrassed.'

'You mean, you're somebody famous whom *I* ought to have known?'

'No, no, nothing like that. It's just my name.'

'Well . . .?'

'It's Dawn,' the girl said. 'Dawn Winterbottom.' Otterburn grinned. 'You did promise,' the girl said.

'No, no,' Otterburn said. His smile broadened. He could not suppress a chuckle. The girl's colour was up as she looked at her plate. Otterburn found himself reaching over to touch her hand.

'Please. Don't be offended. I'd probably have found nothing funny in it if you hadn't so obviously expected me to. Please,' he said again, when she didn't respond. 'Finish your spaghetti before it goes cold, and don't mind me.'

The girl took some more spaghetti on to her fork. 'I've

thought of changing it,' she said. 'But after all it is my own name and I think people should make the best of their own names. They're part of them, after all. Aren't they?'

'Of course they are,' said Otterburn, who saw little logic in what she was saying. 'And after all it's the quality of the personality behind the name that counts, isn't it?'

'I suppose it is.'

'And there's nothing wrong with your personality,' Otterburn went on. He was enjoying himself. 'You're good-natured enough to do a kindness for strangers, like letting those people have your table, and unselfconscious and natural enough to sit with another stranger – a man, what's more – and make pleasant conversation without fear of being misunderstood. I'd say all those are qualities very much in your favour.'

'You seem rather specially nice yourself,' Dawn said.

'Oh, there's nothing special about me.'

'Oh, but there is. Writers are special. They must be or there'd be more of them about.'

'There are more than enough already,' Otterburn said. He was sure that must be true.

'Yes, the competition must be frightening. Tell me, do you actually manage to earn a living from it?'

'Well . . .' Otterburn looked a touch bashful. 'I wish I could say I did. But the fact is, I have a private income.'

'Lucky for you. I'm sure that must take a lot of the worry out of it. It means, I suppose, that you can write what you want to write and not just to make money.'

'You're really very perceptive,' Otterburn said.

'And what are you working on just now?' the girl asked. 'If it's not too personal a question.'

Otterburn emptied his mouth, took a drink of his lager, and said, 'I'm writing a story about a man who comes to live on his own in this city. One day he finds a letter pushed through the door with his name on it, which is strange because nobody knows he's there.'

'What does the letter say?'

'It says, "I shall be in the Ferryboat at seven tonight." '

'Is that all?'

'That's all. No signature, no address, no postmark.'

'Is it from a man or a woman?'

'He can't tell. The handwriting may be disguised.'

'And what does he do? I mean, does he just tear it up and ignore it, or does he take it seriously?'

'He can't help being intrigued by it.'

'No, I expect not.'

'Someone's interested in him, you see.'

'It sounds like something out of a spy story.'

'Yes, it does. But he's just an ordinary sort of chap, who certainly doesn't know any official secrets.'

'But he must have a secret of some kind. Perhaps a guilty one from his past.'

Otterburn looked at her with admiration. 'You know, you really are clever. But I'm afraid that's not the answer. He's led a rather dull and totally respectable life.'

'Hmm. So is it a man or a woman who's written the letter?'

'You asked me that before. I don't know.'

'Well, does he go to the . . . where is it?'

'The Ferryboat. Yes.'

'And what happens?'

'I don't know,' Otterburn said again.

The girl frowned. 'But you must know. You're writing the story.'

'But I don't know how it ends,' Otterburn said. 'Not yet.'

'You mean, you've made up this, this intriguing situation, but you haven't worked the rest of it out?'

'Yes.'

'You've set yourself a problem, haven't you?'

'Oh, it's happened before,' Otterburn said airily. 'It'll work itself out if I hang on and be patient.' He was sure he'd read this in an interview with a writer, somewhere. It sounded to him to have the ring of truth.

'Well, I wish you luck with it,' the girl said. She ate the last scraps of spaghetti, put down her fork and spoon and wiped her mouth with her paper napkin. Otterburn pushed aside the remaining third of his pizza. 'You've not made much of that.'

'It's very filling. Are you having a sweet, or just coffee?'

'What about you?'

'Just coffee, I think. I'd like to buy you a sweet, though, if you could enjoy one.'

'No, thanks,' the girl said. 'I'll accept a coffee, though.'

Otterburn signalled a waitress. To his surprise, one noticed him and came immediately.

'Well,' Dawn said, 'this is very pleasant.'

'I'm glad you think so. Tell the truth, I was feeling, well, a bit down, before you joined me.'

'Because your story's not going well?'

'Yes.'

'Are you married?'

'I was,' Otterburn said. 'Still am, actually,' he admitted, 'but separated. What about you?'

She shook her head. 'No.'

'Not had the time, with all that travelling?'

'I suppose so.'

She reached down and brought up her shoulder bag.

'I'm sorry I can't offer you a cigarette,' Otterburn said, 'but I don't use them.'

'Me neither.' She took the small handkerchief and touched it to her nose. 'There's only one thing wrong with this town. The damp air gives me the perpetual sniffs.'

'There's always a snag to everything.'

'Yes.' She put the bag down again. 'You must live alone, then?'

'Yes.'

'Like the man in the story.'

'Yes. What about you?'

'With an aunt. When I'm here.'

'It's good to have a base. Somewhere you can call home. Will you be off on your travels again soon?'

'It depends. You never seem to get anywhere, always moving about. You see a lot, but you don't get anywhere.'

'And with jobs so hard to come by just now.'

'Yes. My timing hasn't been so good, coming back to England in the middle of a recession.'

'You're young enough to see it through.'

'I'm perhaps older than you think.'

'I wasn't asking,' Otterburn said.

The coffee came. Otterburn, drinking through the froth, found scalding liquid underneath.

'Damnation! I'm either burning my mouth or scalding it tonight.'

'Do you feel better, though?'

'In what way?'

'You said you were down before.'

'Oh, I feel much better now.'

He did. He had never met anybody like Dawn Winterbottom before. Here they were, total strangers, chatting as
easily as if they'd known each other for years. He was wondering how he might prolong this evening – could he venture to
offer to buy her a drink? – when she said: 'I've just remembered. There *is* a pub called the Ferryboat, down by the river,
isn't there?'

'Yes.'

'Do you always use real places in your work?'

'It depends.'

'But couldn't that lead to complications?'

'Not until someone reads it. Maybe I'll give it a fictitious
name before then.'

'You said he went to the pub but you didn't know what
happened when he got there.'

'Yes.'

'Hmm. I never knew writers worked like that. I thought
they had it all planned before they started.'

'Well, now you know different.' An idea came to him.
'Look, if you don't mind my asking, what are you going to do
now?'

'You mean when I leave here?'

'Yes.'

'I suppose I was going home. I was supposed to meet
someone, but it fell through at the last minute.'

'Well, what I was wondering,' Otterburn said, 'was if
you'd like to join me for a drink at the Ferryboat. It's just a
stroll from here. Perhaps you could help me to see what
happens.'

'In the story, you mean?'

'Yes. Being there with somebody else might just spark it
off.'

She smiled. 'I must say, I've never been picked up with such
an unusual come-on.'

'Oh, please,' Otterburn said. 'Please, you misunderstand
me.'

'Don't worry. I've defended my honour in tougher places than this.'

'You're making it difficult for me,' Otterburn said. 'And it's all been so pleasant and natural, so far.'

'I was joking.'

'On the other hand,' Otterburn said, 'there *are* some strange men at large, and if you'd rather not.'

She looked at him. 'I think I'd like to.'

'You'll come?'

'Yes. Thank you.'

Their bills were already on the table. As the girl reached again for her bag, Otterburn picked up both of them.

'Let me get this.'

'Oh, I couldn't do that.'

'Of course you can. It's not a fortune, and it's my pleasure.'

Outside, as they strolled towards the pub, she slightly ahead of him on the narrow pavement, Otterburn could not bring her face to mind. It was, he thought, one of those faces which seem to change with the light, one whose features would fix themselves only after another meeting. While her clothes were neat and clean, like her hair and hands, she didn't dress for effect either. She was a tall girl and her heels were not high. Over her jumper and skirt she wore a lemon-coloured lightweight raincoat which she had not taken off during the meal. And what an awkward business it was, Otterburn reflected, simply walking along pavements like this with anybody one didn't know well. The naturalness and ease of the café had gone, leaving him selfconscious, casting about for something to say. She was silent too, now. He took her elbow and turned her as she would have passed the mouth of the alley which led to the river.

'Down here.'

The American car had gone. Otterburn hoped it meant that his wife was no longer inside. He went up on his toes and looked in through the small-paned window. He couldn't see her.

'What are you doing?'

'Looking to see how full it is.'

He would have to risk it. He went in first, then held the door so that she could pass him. The pub's evening was in full swing. All the seats looked taken. The girl followed Otterburn to the bar.

'What will you have?'

'What are you having?'

'I don't know. A Scotch, perhaps.'

'I'd like that. On the rocks, please.' She turned and looked round the room as Otterburn ordered. 'Is this your local?'

'It's the nearest.'

'You live here, by the river?'

'Yes.'

'Is that where the man in the story lives?'

'Er, yes, it is.'

'How many of these people do you know?'

'Just one or two I'd pass the time of day with.'

'Which one would you choose as the writer of the letter?'

'I don't know.'

'Is it a man or a woman?' she asked him, for the third time.

'I don't know.'

'It's really got to be a woman, hasn't it? Cheers.'

'Cheers,' Otterburn said. 'Yes, I suppose it has.'

'Unless you're building up to some kind of homosexual situation.'

'Oh, no,' Otterburn said. 'Nothing like that.'

'Why not?'

'I hadn't thought of that.'

'It might be worth thinking about, though, mightn't it?'

'Hmm,' Otterburn said. He thought about it now as his glance flickered round the room. Could the author of the note still be here, patiently waiting for him but unable to make a move now because he was with someone else?

'Your character's not gay, then? The one who gets the letter.'

'No.'

'You could always make him gay.'

'Hmm.'

'Perhaps he's got latent homosexual tendencies that he's never known about, or kept firmly suppressed.'

'Ye-es . . .'

'And the writer of the letter recognises that.'

Otterburn felt uneasy and offended.

'I don't think I'd like that.'

'Do you find it distasteful? I thought writers were men of the world.'

'It's just that I know very little about all that.'

'Did you imagine it as some woman who secretly fancies him?'

'I've told you, I haven't thought it through yet.'

'I'm only trying to help you, like you said.'

'Of course, but –'

'If it's a woman, why doesn't she simply make it in her way to bump into him and get to know him?'

'Perhaps she's shy and repressed.'

'She's going to be awfully disappointed if she arouses his interest with mysterious letters and then he doesn't take to *her*.'

'Perhaps she doesn't intend to reveal herself.'

'Then why make an assignation?'

'I don't know. He's only had the one letter. Perhaps she'll tell him more in a later one.'

'It's not much of a story, is it?'

'Well, not so far.'

'If you did it the way I suggested, you could make it really strong. You could bring in homosexual jealousy and revenge. Perhaps suicide, or even murder.'

'You've got a very lurid mind.'

'Do you think so?'

There was a glint in her eye. It occurred to Otterburn to wonder if she was pulling his leg.

'Anyway,' he said, 'it's not the kind of story I write.'

'Not so far, perhaps. But perhaps you should widen your scope. Perhaps that's why you're not better known.'

'I'll think about it,' Otterburn said. 'Let's have another drink.'

'Thank you.' She gave him her glass.

When he turned with the refills she waved to him from a table.

'If you don't know any homosexuals,' she said as he sat down, 'I could introduce you to some.'

'Here?'

'Yes. There are one or two in the company at the theatre, to begin with; and some others who live here. They're not all madly camp,' she went on, as Otterburn frowned. 'Some of them you might never guess at, unless you were that way inclined yourself.'

It would mean, Otterburn thought, that he could see her again. He had never met anyone like her. He couldn't read her. She seemed in control of every situation. *He* had seemed in charge for a time, in the pizza place; but not now.

'Well,' he said, 'I'll try anything once.'

She smiled. 'Be careful. I only suggested you meet them.'

Otterburn blushed. 'How long are you staying in town?'

'Until I get bored. Or the money runs out.'

'What do you do when you've got a job?'

'I've done all kinds of things. I was teaching English as a foreign language in Italy. But I was foolish enough to have an affair with the man who owned the school and when his wife found out he ran back to her bosom and I had to move on.'

Otterburn, flabbergasted by her candour, looked at her with renewed interest and said nothing.

'Then I've been a waitress and a barmaid. I've hugged a guitar about and sung at folk clubs and done seasonal work at holiday camps. I worked for six months as a secretary in Australia. I did a stint at a summer camp for children in America; your keep and some spending money and a chance to see a bit of the country.' She shrugged. 'Now I'm here for a while. Till something turns up.'

'You don't sound the type to bring a man his pipe and slippers in an evening.'

'Is that the kind of woman you like?'

'I suppose I've always been used to knowing where I am.'

'You left your wife, though. Or did she leave you?'

'Oh, *I* left.'

'Were you in a rut?'

'Yes. Yes, I suppose I was.'

'But with your work, and your private means, you could go anywhere you like.'

'I suppose I could.'

'Why don't you?'

'I suppose you think of writers like yourself, restless, always on the move.'

'Perhaps I do.'

'They're not all like that. Haven't you heard of the country cottage, with roses round the door?'

'I'd love to read something you've written. Could you lend me something?'

'I left everything behind when I moved out. It was rather sudden and I wanted to travel light.'

'Perhaps I'll look in the public library.'

'I doubt if you'll find anything. My early books are out of print and I've mostly published in magazines since.'

'You need a really good shake-up and a change of direction.'

'That's what I had in mind when I left my wife and came here.'

'It's a start, anyway.'

The whisky was going down very quickly. Otterburn thought he perhaps should have stuck to beer.

'Could you enjoy another?'

'Yes, I could,' Dawn said. She opened her bag. 'But let me get them.'

'No, no,' Otterburn said. 'I'll go.'

'You can go,' the girl said, 'but I'll pay.' She put a pound note on the table.

Otterburn hesitated, then picked up the note. 'Same again?'

'Unless you'd like something different.'

'I hardly like to mention it,' Otterburn said, 'but the prices they charge here, this won't cover it.'

The girl laughed out loud as she put some coins on the table. Otterburn took to the bar the image of her laughing. *Now* he knew what her face was like.

'How do I get in touch with you?' he asked when he came back. 'If I want to take you up on your offer.'

'Are you on the phone?'

'No. Well, there is a communal phone, but it depends on someone answering it and I might not get the message.'

'I'll give you my number,' Dawn said. She wrote on a slip of paper.

They left after another round of drinks, which Otterburn bought.

'Well,' she said, 'I'm afraid I wasn't much help.'

'Oh, these things often take a little time,' Otterburn said. 'Perhaps I'll try thinking along the lines you suggested.'

'Just whereabouts do you live?'

'Along here.'

They strolled along the embankment. It was a fine night. The river slid by. Lights were reflected in its smooth broad surface. Here they were, Otterburn thought, walking by the river in one of the oldest cities in Europe. He felt elated, buoyed up by the beauty, the mystery, the boundless possibilities of it all.

'That's me, up there.' He pointed as they paused before the house. 'Third floor front.'

'Yes,' Dawn said. 'Well, you won't get your feet wet there.'

'Hmm?'

'The river comes up and floods these houses practically every year.'

'Perhaps I shan't be here long, anyway.'

'You're not settled, then?'

'Oh, no. Sort of in transit, really.'

She asked him the time. 'I'd offer to come up with you,' she said then, 'but I really must go.'

'My dear young woman!' Otterburn said.

'What's the matter?'

'I hope you don't say such things to every strange man you meet.'

'There you go again, thinking you're no different from anybody else.'

'You flatter me,' Otterburn said.

'I must be off, anyway. Thank you for a very pleasant evening.'

'Thank *you*,' Otterburn said. 'But won't you let me see you home?'

'No. I can get a bus just across the bridge. Goodnight.'

She was moving away from him, quite rapidly. He called after her. 'Goodnight.'

He let himself into the house and went straight to bed. He thought that he would lie awake for some time, but only a few minutes after he had started to retrace the evening from the moment she walked into the restaurant he fell asleep.

He slept quite late. An idea had formed in his mind and he lay on his back, the house still around him apart from the hum of a vacuum cleaner somewhere below, and considered the sheer audacity of it. In a while he got up, breakfasted on cereal, toast and coffee, washed himself and dressed. He looked for coins, found the paper with the girl's number on it and went down to the wall telephone on the ground floor. He dialled. A woman's voice answered.

'Could I speak to Miss Winterbottom, please.'

'Just a minute. I'll get her.'

'Hullo?'

'Dawn? It's Malcolm Otterburn.'

'Oh, hullo.'

'I was thinking . . .'

'Yes?'

'What you were saying about broadening my scope.'

'Oh, yes?'

'I was wondering how far ten thousand pounds would take us.'

'You were what?'

'We could get quite a long way on that, I should think. Wouldn't you?'

'Pretty well all the way round.' She laughed. 'Are you serious?'

'Oh, quite.'

'Look,' she said, 'I was just going out. I'll see you in the Ferryboat at seven.'

'Will you think about it?'

'Oh, yes. And I hope you will too.'

'I've done that.'

'All right. But I'm late for an appointment so I must rush. I'll see you in the Ferryboat at seven.' She hung up.

Otterburn saw the envelope on the mat behind the front door as he turned from the telephone. He picked it up. It had his name on it. He slit it open and took out the single folded sheet of paper. 'I saw you,' the note said, in the same hand, 'but you didn't see me. I like your new outfit.' He folded it and pushed it into his trousers pocket. Checking that he had his keys, he left the house and walked along the embankment and up into the town. In a branch of W. H. Smith he bought a pad of feint ruled A4 paper and some cartridges for his fountain pen.

Back in his room, he pulled the table over to the window and sat down with the pad of paper before him. He got the ink flowing in the nib of his pen, looked out at the river for a few moments, then rested his cheek on his left hand and began to write:

'Otterburn had come to live in this cathedral city when he left his wife. He rented a room and kitchen, with a shared bath and lavatory on the next landing. He had never lived alone in his life before and from his window he could look down three floors at the river flowing between its stone banks and think that at least he hadn't far to go if he decided to do away with himself . . .'

The Pity of it All

Wednesday afternoon, it was – as if she'd ever forget – half-day closing, and Nancy's mother was going on while she cleaned the house around Nancy, who was doing the week's wash. Since Nancy seldom went out in the evenings and couldn't watch television forever after she had put little June to bed, the house was near spotless before Nancy's mother started on it; but she had to occupy herself and Wednesday afternoon had become a ritual. Nancy's mother came and cleaned the house and went on about something.

What she was going on about now was what she had gone on about ever since Jim had been killed. Where was the sense, she asked, in Nancy tying herself to this house when there was a place for her at home, a garden for little June to play in instead of a short length of street and a deathtrap of a through-road at the end of it, and herself and Nancy's father to look after the child while Nancy went out and enjoyed herself?

Oh, and didn't she go on! Saying the same things, week after week. She had decided what she thought was best, and wouldn't leave it alone.

'I like my independence,' Nancy always told her. 'I like to have a life of my own.'

'You bring June to me on your way to the shop,' Nancy's mother said, 'and you collect her on your way home. You can't go out on a night because she's got to be looked after. If you call that having a life of your own. You never get out and see anybody.'

She saw enough people in the shop during the day, Nancy

always told her. She was happy enough in her own home when she'd done her day's work.

'A young woman like you, shutting yourself off,' her mother said. 'You'll never get anywhere if you don't get out and about.' She would never find another husband, Nancy's mother meant. Jim had been taken suddenly, and that was sad; but Nancy was a young woman, with time to have another two or three bairns, but not if she never went out and mixed with people socially.

It was the first week of the school holidays and children were noisy in the street. Some young ones had been and fetched June straight after dinner. June herself would be starting junior school in the autumn. Then, with Nancy tied at the shop till six in the evening, Nancy's mother would accept the extra chore of collecting June in the afternoon. All the more reason, Nancy could hear her mother saying, why Nancy should listen to sense and sell this house and move back home. But though Nancy had often spoken to Jim of 'popping round home' when visiting her parents' house, she no longer thought of it as such. Here was home, the house she and Jim had bought and done up together, talking of the day they would get something better: a semi, they thought, with a lawn at the back to sit out on and a vegetable patch where Jim could grow things. There had been no rush.

Then they had come to tell her about Jim, baffled themselves by the tragedy of it. In a safe pit with a low accident rate, and no fatalities for years past, he had walked alone into a heading, where a stone had fallen out of the roof, pinning him down and, so they told her as a crumb of comfort, killing him instantly. She was carrying the child and thought at first she would surely lose it. The doctors told her she was tough. Her mother had been known to call her hard. But Nancy had never paraded her feelings; she did not know how to behave to impress others. Her duty was to hang on and think of the new life growing inside her: a bit of Jim that he would now never see. Perhaps she would re-marry one day; but she would not go out and look for a chap, and he would have to be pretty special for her to notice him. That she had told her mother. It seemed to Nancy that she told her every Wednesday, while her mother went on.

Now she was telling Nancy that she'd had a reply from a guesthouse in Bournemouth, whose address a friend had given her, and they could have accommodation for the last two weeks in August. Nancy's mother thought the south coast would be a pleasant change, but if Nancy wanted to go elsewhere with a friend it would be no trouble for her and Nancy's father to take little June with them. But no, there was nowhere else that Nancy wanted to go.

Afterwards, Nancy found she could remember that moment with vivid clarity, though its components were all familiar ones. There was the attitude of her mother's body as she held the vacuum cleaner while she wound the flex on to the hooks; the sudden rush of water in the automatic washer as it performed its last rinse; the sunlight on the step outside the scullery door. The voices of the children were no longer near.

'Just have a look out at June, will you?' she said, as she opened the washer and passed clothes over into the drying compartment. 'They've gone quiet.'

Then a minute or so must have passed, but it seemed like no time at all before Nancy's mother was calling at the end of the yard: 'June! June, where are you? 'Ey, you two, bring June back here. Don't you know how busy that road is? No, keep hold of her! Don't let her –!' And Nancy was out and running across the flagstones and into the street, as though she knew before she heard that awful screech of tyres and saw the car slewed round and the little legs in the blue and white Marks and Spencer socks, washed just once, and the stupid, stupid older girls who had led her into it, standing petrified, soundless, and she herself making no sound – not yet – while her mother set up an endless moaning chant beside her: 'Oh! oh! oh! oh! oh! . . .'

Nancy's father could not eat his food. Nancy had had nothing but cups of tea for over twenty-four hours. They talked behind her in low voices. 'It's the shock,' her father was saying. He couldn't take it in.

Nancy's mother was saying what she'd said ever since Jim died; that there had been no sense in Nancy living on her own with the bairn, when a good home had been waiting for them here. Nancy told her to shut up, let it drop.

'I don't care, Nancy. You could have come here and been as free as you liked. You can't stop living just because – '

'Just because what?' Nancy challenged her. 'What are you talking about? I don't know how you can fashion to bring it all up. You never let things rest; you just go on and on. You were sick to get me out of that house, and now you've got something you can hold against me for the rest of your life.'

'Nancy!'

There might have been a row then, because if what Nancy accused her mother of was not strictly true, her mother talking like that would not help Nancy to stop thinking that if only she had taken her advice little June would not have been in that road at the moment that car came along, and . . . And if Jim had not walked into that heading, or he had come out of the pit into a safer job, and if she had never met him and she'd never had the child.

But the doorbell rang.

Nancy's mother, on her feet, went to answer it, coming back a few moments later to stand, curiously tongue-tied, inside the living-room doorway.

'Who is it?' Nancy's father asked.

'It's a chap, to see our Nancy.'

Nancy's father began to get up from the table. 'She can't see anybody now. Can't they leave her in peace? Some folk . . .'

'No, Cliff, wait a minute. It's the feller 'at . . .'

'Who?'

'He's come to see our Nancy.'

'Who is he?' Nancy asked.

'They call him Daymer. If you don't want to see him, just say so.'

'No. If he's come we can't turn him away.'

'Look, Nancy,' her father said, 'there's no law says you've got to see him.'

And she didn't want to, but he'd come and she must.

Her mother showed him in. 'This is a sorry house you've come to.' That tongue. It could spare nobody.

In the one direct look she could manage, Nancy saw that he was nicely dressed, still young. She wondered if his eyes always looked so hurt, or if it was only because of what had happened. Of what, she suddenly realised, had happened to him.

'Mrs Harper . . . I'm sorry to intrude on you at a time like this, but I felt I had to come. There's nothing I could say that wouldn't be hopelessly inadequate. You do understand that I hadn't a chance of avoiding your little girl? It was over in a flash.'

'Nobody's blaming you,' Nancy said. 'It was an accident. They do happen.'

'It was an accident that took her husband,' her mother told him. 'In the pit.'

His voice was shocked. 'Oh, I'm . . . It sounds worse than useless, Mrs Harper, but if there's anything I can do, anything at all.'

'You can't bring her back, can you?'

No mercy there. Her mother was, in fact, a good-hearted woman. But that tongue . . .

'Have you any family, Mr Daymer?' Nancy asked.

'A boy, Peter. He's away at school.'

'I expect he'll be well looked after there.'

'Well . . .'

'It wouldn't be easy for you to come. I thank you for it.'

'If there's any way I can help, any way at all, please let me know. I'll give you a card and put my private address on the back.'

Her mother took the card. 'Oh, you work at Ross's, do you? I used to know Mr Finch's wife, before she died. We did charity work together.'

'He's my father-in-law. I married his daughter, Elizabeth.'

'A lovely woman, she was, Mrs Finch.'

'Yes, indeed. And now I must go. Goodnight, Mr Frost, Mrs Harper.'

'Is he in his car?' her father asked when her mother came back from showing Mr Daymer out.

'Yes.'

'I don't think I could drive a car again, if anything like that happened to me.'

But, Nancy thought, you'd got to keep going. There were times when you thought you couldn't. But you'd got to.

They sold cigarettes and tobacco and cigars, sweets, and
newspapers and magazines in the shop. Some of the magazines
Nancy was not keen on selling. They had pictures in them of
women with their legs open, showing all they'd got. Sometimes the women had their hands down there, as if they were
touching themselves up. Not that she was prudish herself, but
it embarrassed her when men were embarrassed by buying
them. Some of them were. Some were really brazen about it,
eyeing her up and down as they threw the book on to the
counter, as though she chose them all herself and guessed
exactly what they would like. Still, they were dear and the
owner said they made a good profit. Marjorie, the other girl,
younger than Nancy and not married, thought they were a
giggle, and when things were quiet she would pick one out and
read the letters, which were all about sexual experiences.
'They must make them up, Nancy. Don't you think so?
Honest. It's dreamland. Hey, listen to this one!' Well, they
knew what men were like, didn't they? Marjorie would say.
Jim himself had not been averse to a look and a laugh, though
when it came to the thing itself he'd been easily enough
satisfied so long as he got what he called his 'nightcap' regular.
He was always pretty tired and it didn't last long. It was all
right. She'd loved him and couldn't complain, though just
every now and then she'd find herself wishing for a bit of
finesse, that they might linger, enjoy it for itself, not just for
the end of it. And it had been a long time now . . . Marjorie
had a boyfriend, a cocky lad called Jeff, who sometimes called
in to buy a packet of fags and make arrangements with
Marjorie. When Marjorie couldn't resist telling Nancy what a
smashing lover Jeff was, she nearly always stopped at some
place, cutting off the subject in a way which told Nancy she
was sorry that she hadn't got anybody now. And Nancy
wished she wouldn't, because she didn't want that kind of pity.
It had been a long time . . . But she still missed Jim and could
not bring herself to think of anyone taking his place.

Marjorie's big blue eyes brimmed with tears the morning
Nancy returned to the shop. Nancy had to steel herself to
accept this kind of sympathy. It was natural, but it threatened
the defences she was building along the slow path to days in
which there would be moments when her mind was not

obsessed with what had happened. The nights were the worst, before she managed to sleep; then the mornings when she woke ready for a routine – the kisses, cuddles and chuckles, the dressing of a child's warm plump body – that was no longer there. It was why she was still with her parents: her own house had an atmosphere of expectancy, as though waiting for someone to come back from holiday, or a spell in hospital, and resume life as it had known it.

Sometimes Nancy took sandwiches to the shop – there was an electric kettle in the back room where they could make tea or coffee – but it was nice to get out for a while around midday, and she went for a snack then to the Bluebird Cafe, a clean place run by a Cypriot family, a couple of streets away. This particular day she had gone in perhaps a few minutes later than usual to find it full, and she was standing looking for somewhere to sit when a man she hadn't so far noticed spoke to her.

'Mrs Harper . . .'

It was Mr Daymer, at a table for two, with one of the few empty seats in the place opposite him. She said, Oh, hello, and he asked how she was.

'I was just going to order,' he said. 'Perhaps you'd . . .' There was a newspaper on the other seat and one of those slim zip-up cases for papers, as though he'd been keeping the place for somebody. He reached over and moved them. 'Please,' he said. 'There's not much choice, anyway.'

She thanked him and sat down. As he said, there wasn't much choice, and she couldn't be rude.

'I haven't seen you in here before.'

'No. Do you come in much?'

'Yes, I suppose I'm a regular.' But he knew that. She somehow knew that he'd known. So what did he want with her that he had to pretend things and cap his pretence with a downright lie – she was sure he was lying – when he said, 'I had an appointment in town and just happened to spot this place.'? He tried to smile, but it was a poor attempt. He wasn't easy. But how could he be? In his place she would have run a mile before meet her face to face. So why was she so certain he'd been waiting for her, expecting her to come?

He handed her the menu. 'What do you usually have?'

'Oh, just a snack. Poached egg on toast. Something like that.'

'They've got what they claim is home-made steak and kidney pie, I see. What about joining me in that?'

She told him no, she wouldn't; that her mother would have a cooked meal waiting that evening. She didn't even want the snack now, just coffee, her stomach was all knotted, him sitting there bringing it all back so sharp and clear. But his eyes looked so hurt again she couldn't bring herself to get up and leave him.

'Are you living with your parents now?'

'For a bit. My mother thinks I'll stay for good now. She was always on about it before. I've got a nice home, though. I don't want to let it go.'

'I imagined you as an independent person.'

What did he know about her? He wasn't her class, though his voice was more careful than naturally posh. He was the head of a department coming down on to the shop floor in his nice suit and shirt and expensive tie, as at the firm she'd worked for before she married Jim. His fairish hair was just long enough, touching his collar, for fashion, but neatly cut. Like his fingernails. Neat hands, no oil, pit-dirt ingrained, work scars. A gold signet ring, heavy gold watch and strap. A Rolex. She'd seen them in shops, had once looked at some with Jim before he'd laughed and settled for something reliable at thirty quid with a face she'd thought rather smart. She had it in a drawer at home now. It was easy enough to look at his hands because it was too hard to look each other in the face.

He wouldn't have the steak and kidney pie when the waitress came for the order. No, he said, when Nancy said not to mind her, he wasn't really hungry and, like her, he would have a cooked meal this evening and he only ate a substantial lunch when he was entertaining firm's guests. And then, Nancy thought, he wouldn't bring them to the Bluebird, but somewhere like the Regent or the new motel. And when he had his meal tonight it would probably be nearer eight than half-past six, with sherry or gin before it and a bottle of table wine to go with the food. Mr Daymer had married the boss's daughter, Nancy's mother had told her. Nancy's mother had looked up to the late Mrs Finch. Mr Finch apparently still lived in a big house on the other side of the park. She didn't know whether Mr Daymer was clever or not, but it probably didn't matter. He would be looked after in the firm because of who he'd married. He'd landed on his feet. He'd 'got it made', as Jim might have said. So what did he want with her? Oh, he'd done a terrible thing, but nobody was blaming him. Witnesses had said he hadn't a chance. June had been killed because silly young lasses had got her on to the wrong side of the road and then let her start to cross back on her own. They'd been taking care, had promised to take care, but their minds were too young to make them take care all the time. They knew, and they were sorry: everybody was sorry, but it was done. Mr Daymer was sorry, but, as her mother said, he couldn't bring June back.

Because they had just coffee there was an excuse not to linger. Besides, Nancy thought the management didn't like people taking up tables for coffee when there were others wanting seats for lunch. Mr Daymer asked her one or two questions about her job; did she like it, and did her employer look after her. Then he collected his belongings and went out with her.

'Goodbye,' Nancy said. 'Thank you for the coffee.'

'Please,' he said, 'don't forget. If there's anything I can do. Anything at all.'

'That's all right,' she told him, and then again, 'Goodbye.'

She had an idea that he watched her to the corner, but she didn't like to look back to make sure.

He telephoned her at the shop a week later. As it happened, she was on her own in the back room and answered herself.

'Could I speak to Mrs Harper, please.'

'Speaking.'

'Mrs Harper, this is Walter Daymer.'

'Oh, yes?'

'How are you?'

'Oh, pretty fair.'

'Is Wednesday your half-day?'

'Wednesday, yes.'

'Will you be doing anything then?'

A few weeks ago she could have answered him without hesitation: she would be doing the wash while her mother put the polish on a clean house around her.

'I don't know, really.'

'I wondered if you'd like to go for a drive with me.'

'Oh, well . . . I don't know.'

'We could run out into the country. It'd be a change for you.'

'I suppose it would. But you don't have to. There's no need for it.'

'I'd like to. We could have lunch on the way.'

She said, 'Just a minute,' and laid the receiver down, stepping away from the telephone, to think. She was standing like that when Marjorie came in from the shop.

'Are you still on the phone, Nancy?'

'Yes.'

'Are you all right? There's nothing wrong, is there?'

'No. I'm all right.'

The shop bell rang. Marjorie left her. Nancy heard Mr Daymer's voice, small in the receiver. She took a deep breath and picked the receiver up.

They had said they would meet in the market car-park, where Mr Daymer would be first and watch for her. Nancy hadn't wanted him to call for her at the shop; Marjorie might linger and, in any case, the proprietor always came in at the end of a working day. They were behaving, Nancy thought, like people with something to hide. But it was something better not talked about with others until it was over. Someone had told Nancy's mother that Nancy had sat with a man in the Bluebird. Nancy's mother had seemed pleased, probing for hints of a more than casual acquaintance, until Nancy told her it had been Mr Daymer.

Apart from anything else, Nancy's mother had said then, Mr Daymer was a married man. Nancy asked her if she thought his buying her a cup of coffee constituted grounds for divorce. No, said her mother, but it wasn't a big town and people liked to talk. Nancy had told her mother she might fancy the pictures this afternoon and her mother had said that might do her good, help to take her out of herself. Marjorie had seen the film in question and talked about it in some detail.

Mr Daymer took her into a white pub on a hillside on the way. He wanted to buy her a good lunch, but all she would have was a ham and salad sandwich and a glass of lager. When she asked him how he had managed to take the afternooon off, he told her that he would be driving up to Newcastle when he left her. They were building a factory there. She supposed he was important enough not to have to account for every hour of the day. He said he would also take the opportunity of calling to see his son, who was at a boarding school in North Yorkshire. Peter had been writing home about bullying in the school. Mr Daymer's wife, who had experience of boarding school, thought the lad was exaggerating; but Mr Daymer, who had not been away from home until university, felt that the boy was genuinely unhappy and wanted to get him transferred to a day school near home. He believed anyway, he said, that children should spend their formative years with their parents. Then he seemed to become embarrassed by talking about the boy, and changed the subject.

They drove on, arriving eventually at a hill top from where, Mr Daymer told her, you could look into three counties. Or you could, he said, before local government reorganisation had changed so many county boundaries. He wasn't sure where they were now officially. It was very beautiful, though, and they were lucky with the weather.

'I remember,' Mr Daymer said, 'when I was a boy and I got my first bike. A second-hand "sit up and beg" it was. I attached myself to a local cycling club and they came up here one Sunday. It was a matter of pride with me to stay the course. Thirty miles here and thirty back. I slept for twenty-four hours solid after it. My parents thought I'd gone into a coma.' It sounded to Nancy as though Mr Daymer's parents had been no better off than her own. He was a poor boy who had married a rich girl, and there were things they didn't agree about. She wondered who most often had the last word. But now she had to get matters straight.

'Will you tell me something, Mr Daymer?'

'What?' he said. 'But look, I wish you'd call me Walter. Mr Daymer sounds so stiff and formal.'

She couldn't bring herself to do that, so she just said, 'Will you tell me why you wanted to see me again? Why you asked me to come out for a drive with you?'

'It's not an easy question to answer.'

'You must have a reason and I'd like to know what it is. It seems to me I ought to be somebody you'd be best off forgetting.'

'It can't do you much good seeing me, if it comes to that.'

'No.'

'It's just,' he said after a minute, 'that I feel so . . . so inadequate. And sorry for you.'

'I don't need your pity.'

'It's not pity. Not in the ordinary way. Anyway, why did you come? You could have refused easily enough.'

She thought about that before she answered. 'Perhaps I'm sorry for *you*. You can't stop thinking about it, can you?'

'No, I can't,' he said. 'I want to help you and I can't. There's nothing I can do. You know, even a simple thing like a holiday. If you wanted to, I could arrange it.'

'I don't want your money. And there's nowhere I want to go.'

'No. Forgive me. It was a foolish idea.'

'What does your wife think about it? You've told her you've seen me, I suppose?'

'She knows about the other time. I told her what I've told you – that I feel helpless. I thought that first time that you seeing me as a person might help you to get some kind of perspective on it. That it might help you to forget the stranger – the instrument almost – who knocked down your little girl.'

She found herself looking at the interior of the car she was sitting in as a thought turned her suddenly cold. Was it the same colour? 'This isn't the . . .?'

'No, no,' he said. 'I got rid of it.'

She let her breath go. 'But you made it in your way to see me that other time, didn't you?'

'Yes,' he admitted. 'Yes, I did. And I wondered afterwards, I wondered whether it had done either of us any good. Because' – his hands were trembling now: she felt that his whole body was trembling, and he was breathing like somebody who had just run up a flight of stairs – 'because,' he forced himself to say, 'when I think about you now I feel such an overwhelming tenderness and compassion, I can hardly hold it in.'

She began to cry then. He turned and shifted over in his seat as the tears came. 'Nancy . . .' He reached for her and pulled her close to him, his hand stroking her hair, and saying, 'Nancy, Nancy, please don't cry. I don't want to make you unhappy. That's the last thing I want. Please don't cry,' while, at last, she did cry; she cried and cried, as though her heart would finally break.

She cried because of what was past and because she saw with prophetic clarity what was to come. He needed her because of what he had done to her. He could not live with that without knowing her, and she could not turn him away until a time came, as it must, when he would have to go. She would move back into her own house and he would come to her there. Shyly, gently, with a romantic yearning, he would reach for her, and she would take him into her bed. He would be gentle there, too, soft with gratitude for the forgiveness of her body; and she would enjoy that, because it had been a long time for her. He would speak then of love, and the possibility of leaving his wife, disappointed at first, then grateful without knowing it, that she would not respond in kind. For something would happen. She did not know when, she did not know what. But something would happen and when it did she would tell him that he was not her man (he was not strong enough for her, though she would not tell him that). He need not be afraid she would cry for him; she had only ever cried for one man and he would never come back, and must he be hurt because she was not hurt again? Did he not want the peace of knowing that he had needed her for a time as she, she would say, had needed him, but that now it was done it was done? Was there no strength to be drawn from that, or was his heart one made for haunting? All this, she saw, would happen before she was alone again; though as she was the stronger and knew what was to come she would in that way be alone all the time.

They sat apart again. Perhaps, after all, she thought, as he did not speak, he would find the strength to draw back now. Unnoticed, a darkening sky had piled up behind the car. Rain

suddenly lashed the windows. Nancy shivered. Mr Daymer
put his hand in her lap. She answered its pressure with the
pressure of hers. Then, knowing full well how it must, must
end, she waited for it to begin.

The Glad Eye

When his wife threw Talbot out of the house because she suspected him of screwing around and he finally stayed out the best part of the night a couple of times as if to confirm it, he shrugged and told his friends he was sick of married life and had left her. Which in one way was true, since she had offered him the choice of changing his ways or going, and when he wouldn't promise, but denied everything in a defence that climbed from baffled innocence to blustering outrage, it ended with his packing a single bag and storming through the door.

Doreen thought she had handled herself extremely well. Though she was screaming inside, she had refused to be drawn into even raising her voice. All the same, he had gone. She had not expected that. She had seen herself shaming him, then, just possibly, in her own good time, forgiving. It couldn't be all that serious, because she could not understand what he was looking for outside that she didn't give him. Not that she was not bitterly hurt: all the time they had lived together while he was getting rid of his first wife, close and snug; and then, when they'd not been married two minutes, he started this, going out when she was on late shift at the petrol station and not coming home before dawn. The sheer barefaced cheek of it took her breath away. So, surprised but implacable, she let him go.

Talbot took temporary lodgings with a workmate, a married man with two children, who had a spare bedroom. Hollins's wife, a quiet woman, looked sideways at Talbot, but said nothing. Hollins himself, dismissing Talbot's initial explanation, told him he should either never have started playing away, or shown more sense in covering it up.

'Mick,' Talbot said, 'I got pissed a couple of times and kipped down here.'

'First I've heard about it,' Hollins said. 'Is that what you told her?'

'I tried, but she wouldn't have it.'

'And it's what you want me to say if she ever asks?'

'Would you?'

'Nay, lad, *I* might, but I can't speak for the wife. And where *were* you, as a matter of interest?'

But Talbot's face closed up.

He had met his first wife again after a long interval, running into her on the street in Leeds one day when he was buying discount spares for his car. They were face to face before either saw the other and then, though he might have gone on with a muttered word, she stood her ground and appraised him with that oblique dry look he knew of old, that look that said *she* had no illusions about him, so he needn't try it on with *her*. He'd liked that when they met the first time, when she let him see she was interested. No pussyfooting about with her: she let you see what she wanted. And look where it had got her.

'How're you keeping, then?'

'I'm okay.'

'You've shaved your moustache off.'

He touched his bare upper lip. 'Aye.' He had worn it because he had such a baby face: that soft skin, those deep-set blue eyes.

'Grown up a bit, have you? Don't feel you need it to hide behind now?'

'It's a change.'

She had liked it. 'Got married again, did you?'

'Oh, aye. What about you?'

'Me?' She laughed and shook her head. 'Not me.'

'I wondered.'

'Did you? I heard you were living with her.'

'Oh, we were. Before.'

'It can't have been long enough to sort you out.'

'How d'you mean?'

'Before you put a ring on her finger.'

'She knew what she wanted.'

'If not what she was getting.'

'T'same thing.'

'Oh, no,' she said, shaking her head again. 'Never in this wide world.'

'There's no use you starting slagging me now.'

'No, it's got nothing to do with me now. Are you working?'

'Aye. What about you?'

'I am at present. No knowing how long it'll last, though, things being the way they are.'

'They'll pick up.'

'So folk keep saying. Voting Conservative now, are you?'

'Things are bound to pick up.'

'Because they can't get much worse?'

'I just bat on, get me work done.'

'You always were a grafter, I'll say that much for you.'

'Anyway, so you're all right?'

'Yes, I'm all right.'

'Got a chap?'

'Mind your own business.'

'Summat suits you.' With some of the old ease, he reached for and nipped gently the narrow roll of flesh under the T-shirt above the tight waist of her jeans. She took a step back.

'It's being rid of bother that suits me.'

'You're letting yourself go.'

'Not me. That can come off any time I like. Your ways kept me down to skin and bone.'

'There you go again with your slagging. Still can't admit there were faults on both sides.'

'Oh, I don't know why I waste my time talking to you. You'll never change.'

But he liked that extra flesh on her, that soft roundness.

'Anyway,' she said, 'I'm glad I bumped into you, because I've a bone to pick.'

'What's that, then?'

'You owe me some money.'

'How's that?'

'You had a maintenance order made out against you. I've never had a penny piece.'

He affected surprise. 'I signed a banker's order. You should have got it regular.'

She grinned. 'Banker's order. Whenever did you have a bank account? Cash in hand, that's what you always believed in.'

'Anyway, you're managing, aren't you?'

'Yes, I'm managing. And you can stuff your maintenance, for what it's worth. I only asked for it on principle.'

'Well then, there's no need to get bitter about it.'

'Bitter? You don't know the meaning of the word. You lead a charmed life. Folk let you get away with murder. Is *she* soft like that an' all?'

'She looks after me and I look after her.'

'Just like we were, eh?'

'We had some good times.'

'Were they worth it, though?'

'You didn't seem to think so.'

'No. You can only stand so much. Then you want to get rid and start clean again.'

'Where's it got you, though?'

'I'm my own boss. I can come and go as I like. And I don't spend half my time wondering what you're up to.'

'It must be lonely, though, isn't it?'

She caught the look in his eye and took his meaning.

'I don't have to have a chap at *any* price.'

'So you haven't got one at all.'

'Who said so? I told you before – mind your own business.'

She moved, stepped round him. He stood aside. They had exchanged positions when he said, 'Are you going straight home?'

'I might be, I might not.'

'Are you on the bus?'

'I shall be, when I'm ready.'

'I've got the car on a meter round the corner. I'll give you a lift.'

'You've no need.'

'It's on me way. Come on.'

With all the appearance of his old assurance, he walked away from her and turned the corner without looking back. He was opening the passenger door of the old pale blue Ford when she came up behind him.

'How long have you had this?'

'A couple of weeks. I gave a bloke fifty quid for it. It was always letting him down and he couldn't knackle with it like I can. It misses a bit, but I'll get it right.'

He was turning the ignition key, but the engine wouldn't fire. He got out, lifted the bonnet and touched something under there, coming quickly back round and catching the engine on the throttle as it throbbed into life.

'Flooded.'

For some reason then he turned his head and gave her the direct open grin she remembered from the first time she had ever seen him, and for a second it was as though all that had happened between then and now had never been. But it would always be the same with him, she thought. As with his cars, so with his women. He would knackle and fiddle, patch and make do, and grin as he had grinned now, happy in the moment of temporary triumph. Something told her to get out now and leave him, but before she could translate it into desired action he had the car in gear and was moving off.

She began to direct him as they left the city and entered the built-up fringe which joined it to its satellite towns.

'I know the way.'

'No, you don't.' He looked at her. 'Not any more.'

'You've moved?'

He didn't ask where or why, but, driving where she told him to, changed the subject.

'What do you do with yourself?'

'What d'you mean?'

'Do you get out much? I mean to discos or pubs and such. You used to like your nights out.'

'Oh, yes. I'm not missing out on anything.'

'Aren't you?' This time as he twisted his head his look had in it more than idle curiosity.

'Watch the road.'

But it was there, in his mind, uppermost, unavoidable now, what he had wondered only moments after he'd met her, when he noticed that new and appealing fleshing out of arms and breasts. Who had she been with since they parted? How many? How often? Because he remembered how it had been with her, especially when she was at her best, soft, receptive, then mountingly demanding as giving joined with taking, after those laughing evenings round at the pub, and half a dozen martinis topped off with maybe a brandy and Babycham.

'I've been going to evening classes,' she said all at once.

'Evening classes? What to learn?'

'Conversational Italian.'

'What for?'

'I went on holiday to Italy, with a friend.'

'A friend?'

'A pal. I thought it would be nice to know a bit of the language for when I went again.'

'You liked it, did you?'

'Yes. All that sunshine. All them old buildings.'

'All them cheeky fellers.'

'Oh, they're all right. They reminded me of you.'

'How's that?'

'They're full of themselves. They think they can pull women like picking apples off a tree. Especially foreign women, on their own.'

'They specially fancy blonde women, an' all, I've heard.'

'Oh, yes. They're not above pinching your bottom to show it.'

'Cheeky bastards. Are they any good when it comes to the crunch?'

'What do you mean?' She asked, though she knew very well.

'I mean in bed.'

'You'll have to ask somebody else about that.'

'Will I?'

'I don't go abroad to get laid by somebody I've never seen before and won't see again.'

'You can get that at home.'

'I can get what I want at home and leave alone what I don't want.'

'Let's hear you say something in Italian, then.'

'*Vada tutto diritto.*'

'What's that mean?'

'Go straight on.'

'Hey, that sounds real!'

'*Prenda la prima a destra,*' she said after a moment. 'Take the first on the right.'

From the road by the complex of six-storey flats there was a view into the valley, and the estate where they had lived together.

'How long have you been here?'

'Six months. I swapped a three-bedroomed house for a one-bedroomed flat. There seemed more sense in it.'

'You didn't fancy going home to your mother?'

'Oh, no, I value my independence. What's your place like?'

'A two-bedroomed modernised terrace house.'

'Are you buying it?'

'It's hers.'

'She must be the thrifty type.'

'An aunty left it to her. But she's a good manager.'

'Lucky for you.' She spoke again with one hand on the door catch as he reached for the ignition key. 'You've no need to switch off, 'cos you're not coming in.'

'Did I say I wanted to?'

'Well, that's all right, then, because you're not. *La visita è finita.*'

'You mean you can't even thoil me a cup of tea, for old time's sake?'

'Not even a cup of tea. Your wife'll be waiting for you.'

'Oh, she goes out shopping with her mother Saturday afternoons.'

'Well then, you can go and be getting the tea ready for when she comes in.'

'You know,' he said, 'just because we couldn't hit it off living together doesn't mean we can't be friendly.'

'I haven't tried to scratch your eyes out, have I? I should say that's friendly enough, considering.'

His sigh was loud. 'We had some good times at the beginning.'

'And some bad times at the end.'

'It's a pity, though, when you think about it.'

'Look,' she said, 'we agreed to differ. We parted. I've picked up the pieces. You're married to somebody else. So what's your game? What are you after now?'

'There's no game. I'm only trying to be mates.'

'On your bike,' she said. 'On your bike, Des, lad.'

She opened the door, got out, left him, walking to the building without looking back. The lift doors were closing on someone else as she entered the vestibule, so she walked up the two flights to her flat. There she unlocked her door, put her bags in the kitchen and then, before unpacking them, walked into the living-room and to the window which looked out on to the road. The car was still there and he was out with his head under the bonnet again. In his brilliantly white newly laundered shirt of the type he always liked to wear in his leisure hours, sleeves turned back, three buttons open at his chest, impervious to the chill in the day, he looked like someone meant for a warmer climate, and he reminded her once more of the Italian men and the saunter of their lightly clad bodies, at expansive ease in sun and air. Then, as though he were acting out the part for her benefit, he stood away from the car with his hands on his buttocks before looking up and, seeing her, spreading his arms in a huge gesture of resignation.

'Now what's up?' she said aloud, as he pointed first to himself, then to her, and began to walk towards the building. 'Oh, God, he's coming in.'

He was on the landing, trying to get his bearings, when she went to the door.

'What do you want now?'

'I've sprung a leak,' he said. 'I can fix it, but I'll need a bucket of water to get me home.'

He advanced on her before she could speak, as though her allowing him in now was the most natural of courtesies and not even worth a request. She thought for a second of stopping him and telling him to wait; then, as he put his hand on her arm and turned her through the doorway, she went without protest.

She told herself afterwards that it was when she heard the door shut behind him she knew he was back in her life. A part of her was astounded that she couldn't resist, that she could not summon again the spirit with which she had first refused to ask him in; but that part could only observe now as the rest of her, as though hypnotised by the inevitable, waited for the clinching move. 'If it doesn't come,' she told herself, 'I'm safe. I can send him on his way and no harm done.' But she knew with a certainty she would have risked her life on that it would.

He crossed to the window and was standing where she had stood to watch him.

'It's all right here,' he said.

'*I* like it.'

'Doesn't it get the sun?'

'In the evening. I'm not bothered about during the day. I'm out then.'

'Aye,' he said, 'it's all right. Cheaper than the house?'

'A bit.'

'Aye,' he said again. 'Got to watch the pennies. No sense in chucking money away.'

'I don't know if I've got a bucket big enough,' she said.

'I can always make two trips. Just so's I can fill up and get home without boiling.' He followed her into the kitchen. 'You wouldn't have such a thing as a length of insulating tape?'

'I don't think so. I'll have a look.'

She had put her yellow plastic bucket into the sink and was running water into it. Now she bent to a cupboard below and took out her box of odds and ends: screws, nails, curtain hooks, a small screwdriver.

'No, it doesn't look like it.'

'I'm sure there was a roll among the stuff I left.'

'Oh, I've had a clear-out since then. I threw a lot of stuff away when I moved here.'

'You should allus keep a roll of insulating tape. It's one of the handiest things about a house.'

'Like a man,' she heard herself saying, 'but I've managed without one of them.'

'Well, look; if you ever need a job doing 'at you can't manage yourself . . .'

'You mean I can ring your wife up and ask her to send you over?'

'I'm only trying to be friendly.'

'You said that before.'

'I meant it. I don't harbour any bitterness over what you did; all that's in the past.'

'Over what *I* did?' Her laugh was short and bitter. 'God! That's rich, that is. Watch your bucket.' She made to pass him and leave the confined space of the kitchen; then, a moment later, without any seemingly deliberate movement, but like something subtly choreographed and accomplished before the eye could follow, he had her trapped behind the door. 'You're a buggeroo, aren't you?' she said. 'A first-class buggeroo.'

'Sandra . . .'

'Oh, you remember my name as well now? That's the first time you've used it this afternoon.'

'Sandra . . . I've thought about you a lot, you know.'

'You're a bloody liar. You'd have walked straight past me in the street if I hadn't stood in your way.'

'Only because you took me by surprise. I was a bit . . . well, embarrassed.'

'I'll bet you can't remember the last time. And for God's sake watch that bucket. You'll have it all over the floor.'

He reached behind him without stepping away from her and turned off the tap.

'Sandra . . . there's no need for all this.'

'Oh, bloody hell,' she said as she felt his hands on her. 'God, I ought to have my head examined.'

Some time later she reached cigarettes from the bedside cabinet, lit two and handed him one.

'I shall have to get rid of some of this weight.'

'What for? Why do women no sooner get a bit of what a feller likes, they want to get rid of it?'

'It's this spare tyre, though. It bothers me.'

'Do some exercises for it, then.'

'Only solution. If I slim for it I shall lose it off my tits and arms as well.'

'You don't want to do that. They're just right now.'

'You noticed, didn't you? As soon as you saw me. You noticed and you thought, there's old Sandra all fattened up for a quick kill.'

'I thought nowt o' t'sort.'

'What did you think, then?'

'Well, I noticed. I hadn't seen you for three years, so o' course I noticed.'

'Then it struck you while we were talking that you fancied me, so you thought you'd see if there was anything doing.'

'I never really stopped fancying you.'

'You bloody liar. You lie like breathing.'

'Are you trying to kid yourself now you didn't enjoy it?'

'Enjoy it or not, I shouldn't be here like this with you.'

'But you did enjoy it, and you are here, so stop reckoning you wish it hadn't happened.'

'Won't she be wondering where you are?'

'I told you, she's with her mother.'

'You've not got her pregnant yet, then?'

'No.'

'Maybe it was you after all, then, the reason we didn't have any.'

'I'm not ready for a family yet. There's plenty of time for all that.'

'It'd be funny if you'd managed it with me, this time, wouldn't it? That'd be a laugh.'

'Why don't you relax and stop nattering yourself?'

'I can't.' Suddenly she was crying. 'Oh, God, all that time, all that trouble. I knew I should never have stopped when I saw you. You were walking on and I should have let you. I thought I'd got over it and now here we are again.'

'Give up,' he said. He slid his arm back under her head and turned her towards him.

'I don't want any more trouble.'

'There'll be no trouble.'

'There won't because you're not coming here again. I hope you understand that.'

'We'll talk about it later.'

He stroked her shoulder. Behind his closed eyelids he was stroking Doreen. He had watched her as she slipped off garments, seen the shadows as they shaped her body. In a moment she would be with him. She knew when he watched her like that and she slowed her movements as if deliberately making him wait.

He moved, twisted, then straddled and covered her.

'Oh, God, no!' Sandra moaned. 'Don't say you can do it again so soon!'

They were demolishing three blocks of old property in the middle of the town. There were two huge deep square holes with a tall temporary fence round them. Des stood by his lorry, taking a few minutes out for a smoke while the JCB turned on its caterpillars and loaded broken masonry from the third site. Everything around was thick in dust. Fresh clouds of it rose and settled each time the shovel dug and took its load. Hollins came up, crowbar in his hand, and spoke to Des through lips caked with it.

'You what?'

Hollins leaned in and raised his voice against Des's ear. 'I said isn't that your missus over there?' He notioned with his head.

Beyond the piled rubble two women were walking along the road between this site and the fence enclosing the next. One of them was Doreen.

'Haven't you seen her lately?'

'No.'

'I thought you'd been back to try and make it up.'

'You know what she did, don't you?' Des said. 'She changed the locks on the doors so's I couldn't get in.'

'She doesn't spend all her time in the house, does she?'

'No, but if she feels that strong about it I'll be buggered if I'll crawl.'

'Got another nest to keep warm in, anyway, haven't you?' Hollins stood beside Des and watched Doreen and her friend. 'Smart lass, though. You know how to pick 'em, if not how to keep 'em. Look, they're off in for a drink.'

The two women were going through the front door of the King's Arms.

'Look, Mick,' Des said, 'cover for me for five minutes, will you?'

'He wants this load away before dinnertime, doesn't he?'

'Get it filled. I'll be back. If he turns up, tell him I got taken short for a crap.'

He walked towards the pub and went in through the side door. The landlord came out of the Gents in the passage as Des looked at the signs on the doors.

'Tap-room for you, lad, if you're wanting a drink.'

Des went into the big room at the back, where there was heavy linoleum on the floor and the stools and benches were covered in crimson leatherette. No upholstery or carpet for his clothes and boots to soil.

'Give us a pint of lager.'

He usually drank only tea during the working day and he

swallowed a third of the cold liquid before setting the glass down again, feeling it cut through the dust in the back of his throat.

There was a way through from this bar to the one in the lounge and he could see chairs and tables, but no one who was in there.

'Are there two young women in yonder?' he asked the publican.

'Aye. Just come in.'

'There's one in a brown frock with like big yellow flowers on it. Tell her there's somebody in here wants to talk to her, will you?'

As the landlord went through he moved along the bar counter to where he would be out of view if Doreen looked across. He glanced round the room. There was no one else except two middle-aged men at a corner table, making up betting slips for the afternoon's races.

The door opened.

'Oh, it's you. I thought it must be.'

'Doreen. I saw you go by.'

'What do you want, then?' She turned her head and looked at the two men, her voice restrained, low-pitched. She hated scenes.

'I want to talk to you.'

'Get talking, then.'

'I can't here, like this. Are you working tonight?'

'What difference does it make to you?'

'Look, I've only got a couple of minutes before the boss is on me back. Can't I come round and see you?'

'What for?'

'I want my tool kit.'

'I'll leave it out for you.'

'I want to say I'm sorry.'

'So now you've said it.'

'Give us a chance, Doreen, love. Is this all it meant to you, two minutes' talk in a pub?'

'You know what it meant to me. But you didn't give tuppence for it.'

'Well, I do now.' He swallowed the rest of his drink. 'Look, I shall have to go now. If I lose this job I don't know where I'll get another. I'll come round tonight, about eight o'clock, and we'll have a talk.'

'I don't know what there is to talk about.'

'Give us a break, lass. I can't carry on like this.'

'You should have thought about that before.'

'Christ, you're hard! Have you no feeling?'

She hesitated, glanced at the two men once more. 'I'd made my mind up it was finished.'

'Well, if it is, it is. But at least let's talk about it like two grown people.' He looked at her, knew he was at his most abjectly appealing, and waited while she wavered before his direct conscience-stricken gaze.

'Come round if you want, then. But make it half-past seven. I've somewhere to go later on.'

Sluiced clean from head to foot and dressed in a newly washed shirt and his best fawn slacks, he arrived at the door ten minutes early and waited for her to answer his ring. She had changed into sweater and cord jeans. Her make-up looked fresh and he followed her into the living-room on a hint of perfume.

'I haven't got long,' she said.

'Why'd you change the locks?'

'Because I thought I'd very likely come home one night and find you tucked up in bed.'

'It's a job when a bloke can't get into his own house.'

'My house. It was mine before you came and it's still mine.'

'Well, *our* home.'

'A lot you cared for our home, or our marriage.'

'Look, Doreen, I didn't come here to argue. We've had all that. I know I've been a rotten sod . . .'

'Oh, you're admitting it now.'

'Yes, I am. I've been a rotten sod and I want to say I'm sorry and see what we can work out.'

'You mean to say you're admitting you'd been with another woman?'

He sighed. 'Aren't you going to ask me to sit down?'

'Please yourself.'

He was carrying a four-pack of lager. 'Do you want a drink?'

'Not specially.'

'Do you mind if I have one? I'm not finding this easy.'

'Confessing your sins?' He didn't answer. 'You know where the glasses are.'

He went to the kitchen, took two glasses, opened one of the cans and poured into each.

'Here, you may as well join me.'

'Put it down.' He placed the glass on the low table in front of the sofa. The gas fire was on low heat. The room was warm to him. She had always liked more warmth than he did.

'I asked you a question. You didn't answer.'

'What was that?'

'I said, are you admitting now that you'd been with another woman.'

He shook his head. 'I can't deny it. I should have owned up before you threw me out.'

'Why didn't you, then?'

'Because I was scared you wouldn't understand.'

'What makes you think I will now?'

'I don't know. But I've got nothing to lose now, so I thought I'd chance it.'

She shook her head as he offered cigarettes.

'What was she like?'

He shrugged. 'She was nobody.'

'Was she a whore?'

'Hell fire, no! She was a divorced woman. She was a bit, lonely and willing and, well, I was tempted.'

'What was so special about it?'

'Nothing.'

'Have I ever refused you?'

'No.'

'So what did you want from her that you weren't getting at home?'

'I don't know. Ask other fellers; they might explain better than me.'

'I'm not interested in other fellers. I'm asking you.'

'Doreen, love, look, listen.'

'I'm doing both.'

'Look, if a marriage is going to break down as easy as that, it's about time people stopped getting married.'

'A lot of people are. I only wish I'd been one of 'em.'

'I know I can't expect you to take me back straight away . . .'

'If at all.'

'. . . but I have said I'm sorry. I've come here tonight, cap in hand, to try to save our marriage.'

'You'd better tell me how you intend to do it.'

'Well, like I say, I can't expect us to pick up now as if nothing'd happened, so what I thought was if we took a bit of time over it and saw each other for a while without living together, we might get things sorted out.' She reached for the glass in front of her, lifted it, then put it down again without drinking. 'I mean, we could find out how we felt about it after two or three months, or maybe six. P'raps it'd take a year. I don't know, but I'm willing to wait.'

'What do you mean, see each other?'

'I mean we'd be separated, but I'd come and take you out.' He got up and crossed to sit beside her. She moved along the sofa to leave space between them. 'I don't like to think of not seeing you at all, but I do see 'at you'll need time to get over it and make your mind up whether you want me to come back for good.'

'Where are you living now?' she asked after a moment.

'I'm using Mick Hollins's spare bedroom. His wife's a nice woman. I'm comfortable enough for the time being. I mean, I'm hoping it won't be forever.'

'I thought you might have moved in with her.'

'Hell, no!'

'I wish it had never happened.'

'So do I, love. But one mistake. We can't let it spoil everything.' He took her hand and slid his fingers between hers as she instinctively made to pull away. 'What do you say? Where's the harm in giving it a try?' He chuckled and squeezed. 'We can reckon I'm on probation.'

'You can talk,' she said. 'I'll give you that.'

'Somebody's got to talk for both of us,' he said, 'or else that pride of yours'll finish us for good.'

'I call it self-respect.'

'Whatever you call it, you can carry it too far.' He looked at his watch and went to fetch his glass. 'What time are you going out?' he asked when he was beside her again.

'Soon.'

'Is it something important?'

'Why?'

'Chuck it and come out with me. I've missed you.'

'You should have thought of that before.'

'I'm thinking about it now.' He pulled her gently back till their heads were resting a foot apart. 'What do you say?'

'I suppose I can be late.'

'Is nobody calling for you?'

'No. It's some women I meet round at the pub, after bingo.'

'You've never taken up bingo,' he said. 'Not you?'

'No, I meet them after they've been.'

'Well, we could go to another pub and then I could drop you off there for the last half-hour.'

'I don't want them seeing us together, thinking I've turned soft.'

'All right. I can understand that. Till you know your own mind. So let's just stop here and talk a bit more.' He moved his face towards hers. 'Can you manage a kiss on it?'

'You didn't say that was part of the bargain.'

'I didn't think it was till I got you near me. But, you see, I've missed you and there's no reason why we . . .'

He sat up, twisting in his seat. He took a drink, put down his glass, then hunched forward, his arms on his knees. She waited without moving from where he had left her.

'Well, I don't know whether it'll work or not, but we *are* married, even if we shan't be living together, and all I know is I don't want to be tempted to go drinking and birding with the lads at the weekend. And I don't think you . . . well . . .'

'What?' she said.

'I don't think you want to live like a widder-woman either.' He shifted on the sofa and looked at her, taking her hand again, this time holding it between both of his. 'You don't, do you? I mean, let's face it – seeing you, knowing you like I do, it's more than flesh and blood can bear.'

They went, later that evening, to two pubs, neither of them that where she was due to meet her friends. Des chose carefully, knowing the kind of place she liked – or tolerated – and the kind she liked to say she wouldn't be found dead in. He made her laugh a couple of times and for a moment then she could almost forget how he had let her down. For a moment, until her face clouded again and she toyed pensively with her glass while he sustained the conversation single-handed and kept a careful watch on every shift of her mood from the corner of his eye.

He left her a little after one. She awoke from a doze to find him dressing by the bedside. He leaned over to kiss her as he heard her move.

'I'd like to stop till morning,' he said. 'But a bargain's a bargain. Thanks for everything, and I'll be seeing you.'

She had been cold in bed ever since he had left. Now, as she heard the house door shut quietly behind him, she stretched her slack limbs into each warmed corner then, spreadeagled, fell into a deep sleep.

The clack of the letterbox woke her again. She had not slept so soundly for some while. Her body felt drugged with satisfaction. She was surprised that he had gone without argument and thought that she would not, as she'd felt then, have had the will to deny him had he insisted on staying. But this was how it should be. She would call the tune now, until she was sure he was sufficiently contrite and she could take him back. There was, as he had said, plenty of time to consider that. In the meantime, she wished there were someone to bring her a cup of tea.

Des had the Hollinses' youngest on his knee and was helping her with her reading. Bess Hollins, cooking and laying the table for the evening meal, watched them with that slow smile which lingered perpetually, deep in the jet-like lustre of her eyes. It was of a piece with her unhurried movements and her soft Devon voice. She was just beginning to show with her third child.

'I'm sure Uncle Des has had enough of that for now, Claire.'

'Nay, she's right where she is for a minute or two.'

'You're good with them. You should have a family of your own.'

'Not much chance of that, is there, with me placed as I am just now? Anyway, I've got a ready-made family here. What more could a chap want?'

'You're comfortable, are you?'

'As snug as a bug in a rug,' Des said. He squeezed the child. 'I bet you've never heard that one afore, young Claire – "as snug as a bug in a rug". Eh?'

'He is an' all,' Hollins said. He was kneeling on the floor near the sink, with parts of the vacuum cleaner laid out on a sheet of newspaper.

'But look,' Des said, 'I've been meaning to say. I'm taking a lot for granted. I don't want to get under anybody's feet. The minute you feel I'm a bother you've only to say the word.'

'Oh, no,' Bess said. 'Mick and I had a talk about that. You're no trouble to us. You pay your way and the children like you. You can stay as long as you like.'

'But when number three arrives you'll mebbe be needing the room.'

'Oh, it'll be a while before that one needs separate accommodation. And perhaps by then you'll have got your own affairs straightened out.'

'Aye, well. As long as we know where we stand.'

'Might you be going to see your wife tonight?'

'I thought I might pop over later on.'

'He's not saying which one,' Hollins said.

Bess had not heard. She wasn't meant to. It was between men. In the knowing grin that Hollins threw at him over his shoulder there was, with its just discernible glimmer of envy, an invitation to Des to share for a moment his surely understandable glee in the situation he was so cheekily and adroitly manipulating. But Hollins could never remember that cheek was a quality Des only ever recognised in others. For all he gave his friend was that characteristic little frown which Hollins finally understood as the look of one whose cross in life it is to be perpetually misjudged.

And Hollins, turning back to his repairs, thought, 'Well, that must be it, then. That must be how it's done.'

Foreign Parts

He's doing it again. Those two girls passing the pavement table. 'I wonder where they disappear to when they get older . . .' I thought nothing of it when he first brought it up, but now that he's mentioned it again and he's watching them right into the crowd I'm bound to own to a twinge of irritation. No, it's not jealousy: just that after I've agreed to come here and we're together so far from home I don't think he should be looking at other women. Not women yet, either, which is hardly designed to let me forget my own age and the flaws I see in the mirror every day or when I catch a glimpse of myself at that certain angle in a shop window. *For I only have eyes for you, dear* . . . Was that how I imagined it, wanted it? No, come on, Cheryl; we're mature people, worldly enough to plan and take this holiday together simply for the pleasure of it. But still . . .

'There seems to be a particular type of young girl here,' was what he said before. 'They have long legs, narrow hips and full high breasts.' But then, he said, all the grown women you see gossiping in doorways and carrying shopping-bags in every town and village on the island are short-legged, stocky, wide-hipped. So where do all the young girls go? That's like another song . . .

'Do you find them attractive?' I'm asking him now, careful to keep it light and neutral.

'Oh, I'm not really drawn to dark-skinned women. Especially women who don't mature well.' That grin he's giving me before he drinks. He's got the nicest, wickedest grin I've ever seen in a man. What drew my eye the first time I noticed him;

and the way it drives out the sadness that sometimes lurks at the back of his eyes when his face is still.

I don't know what that wife he's separated from looks like, but I can make two compliments out of what he's said – me, the wrong side – if only just – of thirty, with my nearly white hair and my transparent white skin. I can't complain that I don't turn him on. 'You almost glow in the dark,' he said when he saw me on the bed in the heat that first night. Then he was all over me while I lay there, not stopping him but not giving yet, wondering if this was what I'd foreseen at the end of all the white lies and secret planning. But we were both fagged-out from the lateness and the journey and George was over-excited, he said, at that first-ever full sight of me and too quick at the end, for which he apologised. 'It'll be better for you next time,' though it wasn't much, though nice enough and I could see he enjoyed it so I pretended so he wouldn't feel let down.

'It doesn't matter unless you're thinking of something permanent, does it?' Then I chide myself because he could think I'm hinting at him and me.

'I don't follow.'

'Whether they mature well or not.'

'You mean chasing women at their best age? Not really my style.'

'No.' But I don't really know. I don't really know him, come to that. He could still be living with his wife, for all I know; him on one side of London and me on the other and only ever meeting somewhere in the middle. I'm perhaps only one of a string of women he makes up to on his rounds. Except he can hardly go abroad on holiday with all of them. Perhaps I'm just his choice for this year.

The pleasure boats are filling up for trips round Grand Harbour. We've talked about going later. That sea so blue it's almost fierce and the white light that sometimes turns to pink at sunset on the stone fortresses standing on this side of the point and right round the other side. I wondered, I must confess, what kind of place we'd come to that first night, driving from the airport through the dark and nothing to see but piles of white stone all round and the pot-holed roads and the bouncing, swaying minibus that quite turned my stomach over, and me congratulating myself that I hadn't felt a tremor on the plane. But then we woke to the sun . . .

I love the sun: day after day of settled heat without a sign of a thunderstorm or the clouding-over you get at home. But we should be somewhere else, away from this crowded corner of the island, where the streets are narrow and stifling and here on the promenade there's exhaust fumes from the endless traffic churning by. The buses, single-deckers, such as you've not seen in England for a lot of years. George says we send old buses here to die – like elephants all go to that secret graveyard – but the Maltese do them up, painting them in that pale green livery and putting them back into service. Scores of them, you can see, outside the main gate at Valletta. Adaptable, the Maltese, George says. They've learned to be. If everybody at home worked as hard, the country wouldn't be in the mess it is in. Cheap and frequent, too, the buses. Perhaps we should have gone by bus and not bothered hiring the car. As it is, the island being so small, we've seen it all in the first few days, and now . . . No, we're not bored and you do want to relax on a holiday and not spend all your time dashing from place to place; but it does mean we're thrown more on each other.

Head back, the sun on my face, as George goes inside the bar for more drinks. I must be careful. It's fiercer than I'm used to and I go lobster-pink before I brown. What was George saying about nude pin-ups of girls who've been sunbathing in bikinis? They're brown everywhere except the intimate parts and they look as if they've got leprosy in their breasts. Well, he'll have to put up with that, since there's nowhere on this island where you can take all your clothes off. They're devout Catholics here and the women keep covered, which was why when men first looked at me, like those two locals are doing from the table along the pavement, I thought I was perhaps showing a hint of nipple or a too natural bustline without my bra. Until I realised it's my colouring that's the chief novelty. They think I can't see them stripping me where I sit. But I can, and I don't mind as long as I've got my sunglasses to protect me. They're not as brazen as I've heard some Spaniards and Italians can be, so there's no feeling of danger in it. In times gone by, I suppose, I could have been some rich man's favourite and lived in one of those big secret houses in Valletta or Mdina, brought out occasionally to be shown off to his friends, and nothing to do but pamper my body, keep my skin white and not get fat. At home, men hardly look at me twice. I'm just another face in the crowd.

Would I have taken to that kind of life, I wonder? Being kept as a favourite, I mean. I do like men. I like having them around to look after things, make arrangements, take me places. Funny to think I'd have been married to Ronnie now, and perhaps two or three kiddies growing up, if he hadn't got that rare disease they said rats carry. Swimming in that flooded quarry – he loved his swimming, Ronnie did, how he'd have loved all this clean blue water here – when he cuts his foot on a rock and in only a few days he's dead. Of course, I was shocked and I cried and everybody felt sorry for me as well as him, with the date already fixed and the bridesmaids' dresses made. I couldn't tell them – I never told anybody – when I realised a few months later that I'd never really loved him, not as I always think people who marry ought to love each other, and I felt relieved that I'd not gone through with it and found out too late. Though perhaps I wouldn't have found out. Perhaps I should have grown to love him, settled into married life like all the rest, made the best of it. That's living for most people, after all, isn't it?

And as there's been nobody special since, people who remember think I've never got over him, that I must be comparing every eligible man with him and finding them lacking. Well, they are, or else it must be me, because it's never got as far as that since then. Oh, there have been men, and one or two adventures. That time with Mark, when he took me up to Leeds with him because he needed secretarial help, and after dinner and a nightcap he came to my room in his dressing-gown and pyjamas. I'm not on the pill, I told him, and it's the wrong time in the month and I wouldn't risk it like that anyway. And if he didn't have contraceptives in his pocket, ready. I asked him, because I was put out, what had made him think I was such a sure thing, and he said he hadn't been sure at all but it would have been stupid to find I was willing and lose the chance because he hadn't taken precautions in advance. When he smiled, he made me laugh with his little-boy-caught-in-the-jam expression, and I had to admit the sense in what he said. It was nice, too. He was slow and gentle. Though it did cross my mind to wonder afterwards, when there wasn't another time, whether it wasn't consideration that had held him back, but rather when it came to it I wasn't all he'd hoped. But I'm liable to do myself down like that and he *was* awfully busy, always dashing here and there, and it wasn't long before I left for this other job.

George brought his precautions with him, this being a Catholic country and him not wanting the embarrassment of going into a shop and asking, let alone running the risk of being refused. Imagine finding ourselves here, on our own, with a room and a bed for the first time and not being able to do what we came for. Well, partly what we came for. I caught sight of the box when his case was open. Good lord, I thought, taking in the size of it, he can't be expecting it twice every day. But no, he was a bit eager the first couple of nights, then last night he just tucked his arm round me and went to sleep after a kiss. Trust me to lie there then, wanting him to wake up and take me. I nearly got hold of him in the night to bring him on, but I thought better not. If it happens that he can't till he's rested a day or two, it'll really embarrass him. After all, he's not a young man any more. Not an old man, by any means, but over forty. And men have their pride in these matters.

He's a long time coming with those drinks. He'll have got chatting to the barman. Likes to get to know the natives, he always says. I hope those two men don't start thinking I'm on my own and waiting to be picked up. No, I'm obviously on holiday and waiting for someone. They're perhaps hoping it's another woman. I wonder what kind of time two women could have here, if they were that way inclined. Now, I didn't like that. Not the way that one looked then spoke to his friend and they both laughed. I'm not showing anything, am I? So what's the joke?

The joke is, it isn't me they're looking at now, it's this tall girl coming towards us. Blonde. Swedish or German, I'd guess. Nearly six foot, golden brown everywhere you can see. Straight, as though she's carrying a basket on her head, shoulders back, bosom out, free but firm inside her white blouse, and sauntering, sauntering for all the world as if she's on a beach, alone and miles from anywhere. Style. Oh, God, they don't half make you feel small and timid and provincial.

Come on, George, you're missing this one. She's not dark-skinned and she won't disappear as she grows older. She'll still have most of it when she's fifty. No, don't come out till she's gone, even though I want to spend a penny now and I daren't leave the table empty because there isn't another one free.

I'll write that card to my mother. She'll expect more than just the one to say I arrived safely. *We* arrived. Maureen and I. 'I've never heard you talk about Maureen, have I?' she said, because even though the office is miles away and she's never likely to meet any of them I somehow couldn't use any of their names. 'What's the matter with Mavis this year?' 'Oh, she's got a feller.' Which she hasn't. She wanted us to go away together this year like last. 'A friend who lives nearby,' I told Mavis. 'Maureen.' My mother doesn't know that George exists, though Mavis does of course, because him coming into the office every three or four weeks is how I met him. And then when he first asked me out it was when we were alone, naturally, and since he has no reason to tell the others his business, it was more or less left to me to tell them or say nothing. It was because I didn't know his domestic circumstances that I kept quiet. Then I went on like that. Maybe I've got a naturally secretive nature. Or I just believe in personal privacy. Anyway, I didn't feel in need of their advice about the wisdom of going out with a married man, even if he is separated. They'd naturally have thought we were having it off straight away, the minds they've got, and we weren't. We just went out for a meal every two or three weeks and, apart from a kiss or two and some touches a bit more intimate, that was it. No doubt things would have gone further faster if we'd had somewhere private to go, but we hadn't. It was hard enough finding places to park the car so that we could go as far as we did. Which was no doubt frustrating for him, though I liked him for his patience and the way he wasn't desperate to get there at all cost. Or didn't show it.

Then: 'I'm going on holiday, Cher. Like to come with me? To Malta?' And, to make sure I didn't misunderstand: 'We could go as a couple. The only place we'd have to show separate passports would be the airport.'

So he fixed it all. Simply booked a double room through a travel agency. We could have got a flat, which would have meant no fellow guests to size us up, but George didn't want the bother of self-catering and neither did I. Whose business is it besides ours, anyway? People do it all the time nowadays. I brought the cheap ring with me, though. George smiled but didn't rib me about it. 'If it makes you feel easier,' he said. And I have to admit it has. It's a modern world. You don't have to live like an old maid because you're not married. All the same, you don't have to shout it from the rooftops either.

'Here we are.'

'You've been a long time.'

'Did you miss me?' His grin, turning it into a compliment.

Don't nag him, Cheryl. You didn't mean to use that tone of voice. Or did you?

'I was just wondering why it was taking so long.'

'I was chatting to the owner. Likes the British. Makes a change these days. He says he had tears in his eyes as he watched the old *Ark Royal* leave Grand Harbour for the last time.'

'Do you know where the Ladies is?'

'Somewhere inside, I expect. Go in and ask.'

'I don't like to.'

'There's nothing to be shy about.'

'It's the way they look at you.'

'The men? It's your imagination.'

'Oh, is it?'

'You want it both ways.'

'What?'

'You don't like the men looking at you but you're offended when I say they don't.'

'I know when men are looking at me.'

And I do. Like he's looking now. Sidelong. Eyes everywhere but meeting mine. Him and the others. All alike. Not with me any more. Inside himself. Thoughts about me but not for sharing. Not with me, at any rate. Oh God, I wish I hadn't come. I wish I hadn't seen that look. It's gone now, but I saw it. He doesn't know. He doesn't know that I know he can talk about me to someone else. 'Went abroad with this willing piece I picked up on my rounds. Shared a bed in the sunshine.

Nothing serious. All right for a fortnight, but don't want to get involved.'

I'm due to start my period. How can I stay so close to him for another week, share his bed, his bathroom, see him first thing every morning and last thing at night?

'Are you going, then, before we move?'

'Move where?'

'Anywhere you like.'

'I thought you must have somewhere in mind.'

'I'm easy. Where would you like to go?'

'Hampton Court, Kew Gardens, Richmond Park.'

Now why did I say that? He's looking at me now with a little frown.

'Don't you like it here?'

'I was just joking. You said anywhere I liked.'

'There must be something you'd like to see.'

'Haven't we just about seen it all?'

'In less than a week?'

'It's a little island.'

'It seems smaller to little minds.'

'Sorry.'

'Don't mention it.'

'I meant, what did you say?'

'It wasn't important.'

It was, though. And I did hear it. Is that what he really thinks about me? He's good at hiding his feelings. I mean, they don't show in his face. If I have irritated him nobody could tell from his face. But he did say it. Straight out. As good as telling me I've got a small mind. Now when did he come to that conclusion – before we came or since we got here?

He's bored with me, that's what it is. He's lost interest in telling me things. When he notices something now he keeps it to himself. He's saddled with me, all this way from home. He can't make friends, either, without including me. He's probably wishing he was on his own. If he's not now, he will be when I tell him the curse is due. A fat lot of good I'll be to him then. Because that's all he brought me for. It must be.

'Look, do you want me to go and ask?'

'Sorry. What?'

'Sorry or what – which?'

'Sorry?'

He's playing with me now. I always suspected he could have a clever tongue.

'Would you like me to go and find the Ladies for you?'

'No, thanks. I'll go.'

And, of course, like so many little things you think you'll find embarrassing, it's mostly in the mind. The man behind the bar hardly looks at me as he answers the question I don't finish.

'Can you tell me where the – ?'

'Up the steps, madam.'

Yes, I shall probably start properly in the night. I must be careful about the sheets, and I shall have to tell George. Funny, I was half pleased that I wouldn't be bothered with it for a few days – that I had the perfect excuse – but now I'm fancying him, thinking about it, remembering what it was like – or what it would have been if I'd enjoyed it more. Suppose I said I wanted to go back to the hotel now and we went up to the room and I let him see what I wanted and I gave him a really good time, without one of those things, unprotected, nothing between us – surely I'm in the safe period now – he'd like that, wouldn't he? He'd be especially grateful for that.

He's got to be glad he came. He's got to remember it and me, not tip me out of his thoughts like Mark did after that time in Leeds. Oh yes, he did, Cheryl. We know he was here, there and everywhere and you left for that other job, but he could have kept in touch, spared you an hour or two for a meal, or just a drink, showed you that even if he hadn't enjoyed your body enough to want it again there should still be some tender feeling – or at least respect – between people who've been as close as that. Close? Mouth to mouth, skin to skin, flesh to flesh. How close was that, ever? You've been used, they'd say; that type who sit around in baggy frocks and talk and talk about sexist advertising and exploitation and men who look at them in the street, until you think they must live every minute of their lives close to screaming. So why can't I say I used them – Mark and George – that I had them for my enjoyment? I can't because I didn't. They had me, and I let them.

'You're easeful, Cheryl,' my mother says to me when I come home and put my slippers on and curl up near the fire with the telly. 'You never stir yourself. You let everything come to you.' And what doesn't come I do without. That's why she said what she said when I told her I was going abroad for the first time. 'Do you good. Take you out of yourself.' To where?

I wonder what he's thinking – George – as he sits there waiting for me. His bare arm's stretched out as his fingers hold the cold glass on the table. You think they're thin, his arms, but they're strong and the muscle's hard under that down of hair that's almost auburn in the sun. He's lean and hard like that all over, like a board, and not the slightest hint of a paunch. Only in that touch of scrawniness about the neck can you see – oh, ever so clearly when you think hard about it – what he'll look like as an old man, when the adam's apple shows bigger and the skin pulls tight over his cheekbones and round his mouth. His eyes are the kind that will turn paler then and perhaps water at every touch of a cold wind.

Oh, George, who are you? Why are we in this strange place together? What do you want with me? Tell me, George, because I'm lonely.

'There, that couldn't have been so bad. Was it?'

'No.' His humour's back. Perhaps I misjudged him: my imagination reading things that aren't there.

'Shall we go back?'

'To the hotel?'

'Uh, huh. It's noisy and smelly here, with all the traffic. We can lie out on the roof.'

'If everybody else hasn't had the same idea.'

Come on, George, let me surprise you. We'll call in the room to change and then I'll surprise you; and afterwards we'll talk, because it will have been different and you'll know that.

The cars they hire out to you, they're all the same make, George says, all the same colour, all with around 30,000 miles on the clock. And the tyres. George wouldn't accept the car the garage man brought him until that bald front tyre was changed.

'If I as much as drove out of the front gate at home with a tyre like that,' George told him, 'I'd be pinched on the spot.'

'But it's not raining,' the man said, oh so reasonable. Oh so reasonable is what they all are. 'What's the trouble?' they'll say if you find anything wrong. As though sensible men can reach agreement on any subject on earth. But George was firm and the man said to follow him and drove round to a garage in a back street where he took a wheel from an identical car and swapped it for ours. We both laughed when the other car, with our bald tyre, turned up the next day for another guest. 'Are you going to tell him?' I asked, and George said, 'He's got eyes in his head. And, like Mr Whatshisname pointed out, it's not raining.'

There are even more cars outside the hotel now and George says to go in while he finds a place to park. It's a relief to be out of that tin box in heat like this.

'Oh, Mrs Jennings.' The girl at the desk calling. 'Mrs Jennings.'

Nobody's addressed me by any name at all, except madam, so far, and I'm nearly to the lift before it dawns.

'International telegram for your husband. It came just after lunch and I didn't know where to reach you.'

'Oh, right. Thanks.'

It's confusion that carries me on into the lift and up to the room without waiting for George. Who knows he's here? The lift doors again. Sounds carry with all these bare tiled floors. His tap.

'The girl downstairs gave me this.'

'For me? A telegram?'

Turning away to give him a moment of privacy. The sea glinting between the white buildings beyond the dusty road. A family – mother in blue-flowered bikini overflowing with rolls of mahogany flesh, father in trunks, hair everywhere except on top of his head, two small children – crammed, with deck-chairs, on to a sliver of sand. All the sand there is. Always there, every day, foreigners, rude; they stare if you go any-where near them, as if you might march up and ask for your turn.

'It's Kathleen . . .'

Me blank. Who?

'She's been taken ill.'

His wife, of course. Mrs Jennings.

'Is it serious?'

'I shall have to put in a phone call.' George looking round at the telephone as though he doesn't know how to start.

'Who knew you were here?'

'My father. I had to leave word with somebody.'

Because he couldn't cut himself off. He's still tied. He's separated but he leaves word where he is. If not who with.

On the phone now to the girl at the desk. 'Hullo . . . Yes, this is Mr Jennings. I want to make a call to England. It's a London number . . .'

Listening to the number he gives her. Could be anywhere in Greater London, except for the three or four exchanges I happen to know.

George sits on the bed, his back to me. The bed where I was going to give him a good time, something to remember. Why can't I feel for him, for her? Because I don't know her. Mrs Jennings. I don't know him; nothing of all that life of his, past and present, out there. Only a joke, a laugh, some figures of speech, the way he holds his knife and fork, chews food; his smell, his weight and touch in the dark, his spasm and his gasp.

He's telling me nothing. Sitting so still. 'Surplus to require-ments.' That's one I've heard him use. Now it's me. 'Not wanted on voyage.' I won't ask.

'I'll be about downstairs.' If you want me.

Cool lobby with grey and yellow tiles. The girl's face turning from the switchboard, eyes behind huge dark glasses. She knows. They all know. Do they care? None of their business. But I've made it their business by wearing this ring. I care what you think, which is why I'm pretending. Mrs Jennings. No, I'm not Mrs Jennings. I'm me, Cheryl Green, on a dirty fortnight with Mrs Jennings's husband and what's it to you?

If it's serious enough for a telegram, he'll have to go home. Find an early flight and leave. And what shall I do? 'You stay on, Cher,' I can hear him saying. 'It's all paid for and you may as well have the benefit.' Of what? Curious looks? Questions from the bolder or kindlier ones? 'What a pity your husband had to leave.' 'Yes. He was called away on urgent business.' Still living that pretence after he's gone.

But what can I tell my mother if I arrive home a week early myself?

Well, I know what I'm going to do for a start. Get rid of this bloody ring. Not another minute will I wear that.

I'm standing on the rocks between the road and the sea when I hear him call. He waves as he walks towards me.

'Did you get through?'

Why am I asking? He'll tell me what he wants me to know. Just as much. Just as little.

'Yes.' A deep breath. 'She's taken an overdose.'

That quick flick of a glance as he said it, anticipating my reaction, which is something like three seconds of pure naked panic before, with my heart pounding, he says, 'She's all right. They found her in time.'

'Can you get a flight home?'

A shake of the head; something stubborn about the mouth. 'I'm not going. It was a put-up job. She never intended it to work.'

'How can you know that?'

'I know her.'

'All the same . . .'

'She's pulling the string, that's all. Letting me know she's still holding the other end. She didn't want me when she had me – not what I call wanting – but she just can't let go.'

George talking now, letting it all come out, everything he's never told me before. How he went for her quietness, thought she was different, ladylike; found she was just dull, didn't care, went through life in a trance; wouldn't think of a child, but let him take his occasional satisfaction till shame turned him off and he couldn't any longer. Now she was bleeding him dry of every penny she could, living in that expensive mort-gaged house, never lifting a finger to provide for herself, just hanging around till he couldn't imagine what she did all day, what she thought about, how she passed her idle life: a kept woman with no obligation to provide his pleasure.

'She knew where I was. She'd get it out of the old man. He'd soften when she pleaded with him. He'd like us back together. Separation and divorce, they're all against his grain. I can't make him see what she was doing to me. She wasn't unfaith-ful, didn't drink too much. She liked money but she kept things going in a fashion. Why couldn't I make the best of things, look at people who had real troubles?

'Well, in twelve months' time I'll be legally free. And in the meantime I'm not going to let her spoil this.'

'All the same, it won't look very nice, will it? Your wife taking an overdose while you're abroad with your fancy woman?'

'Don't talk like that. Why do you say such a thing?'

'Because . . .' Shrugging. Because it's true, George.

What does he want me to say?

'I can't tell you how much I've enjoyed this. This peace. It's early days yet, Cher, but I'd like to think . . .' Then he sees, as I move my hand. 'You've lost your ring. Have you taken it off? Where is it?'

'Down there.' And, as he looks puzzled: 'In the sea. It floated. I watched it for a while. There's no tide here, is there? It could float there till somebody sees it and fishes it out and wonders how it got there.'

'Did you take it off because of the telegram?'

'Better an honest fancy woman than a counterfeit wife.' I like that: it's well put. I've surprised myself.

'Listen, Cher; I want you to understand. I'm not being callous when I refuse to run home to her. She does need help, but not from me. This is her last throw. When this doesn't work, she'll leave me alone.'

'Why is it so important, stopping on here?'

'Because it's not finished. Because if we go back now I don't think things will ever be the same. It's early days, like I said, Cher. I shan't be free for another year; but I hope when I am you'll still be around. Will you?' Taking my ringless hand, he asks again. 'Will you, Cher?'

And how easy it is once the question's put; once I know exactly what he wants.

'If you really want me to be, George.'

Because I do get lonely, and time is getting on, and I do like having a man around to look after me and take me places; and all the rest I can manage. It's what you give for what you get, and I'll be as fair as I can. There is something I ought to tell him if I were being totally honest, all the cards on the table, and that's that I feel I know his wife now, know her better than I know him (or how could I have been on the wrong tack all this time?). But it's a thing he'll never see just now and with a bit of luck perhaps it'll never dawn on him later. Because I'll be better than that. Oh I will, I will, I will . . .

Huby Falling

I was at school with Clifford Huby. He must be the most famous product of an establishment not given to turning out celebrities or even fitting its sons for much in the way of material success. Huby managed it on both counts: the wealth through a business acumen none of us knew he possessed and the fame through a taste for high living and a second wife who had taken off most of her clothes in a couple of minor films and whose breasts photographed well in a wet swimsuit on the deck of a yacht off the Côte d'Azur. Now notoriety . . .

We were a wartime intake, most of us scholarship boys from working-class homes, with just a few fee-paying pupils among us, of whom Huby was one. Secondary education in those days was limited to the bright and to those who had the cash to compensate for their dullness. Classes were small and everyone knew everyone else. But Huby was never in my set, whose activities often bordered on, and occasionally slipped over into, the criminal. Eddie Duncalf, who, the last I heard of him, was driving a lorry, once went to a party at Huby's house and reported that the guests were mostly boys from the snobbier and more expensive schools in the locality and their standoffish sisters; so I gathered that Huby's family had solid connections. Scholastically, Huby was a plodder. In his relationships he displayed a tactlessness which irritated some to the point of cursing him, and there were instances of reckless behaviour which endangered not only himself but others. Nor was it unknown for him to pick on someone smaller than himself in a manner not so much brutal as foolishly gleeful. 'You don't know your own strength, Huby, you daft bugger!'

Well, he found out. And some of us had already found his soft centre.

Our headmaster was Dr Heathcote Jefferies, a fiery little jumping-cracker of a man whose voice when he was enraged – and he often was – could be heard halfway through the long corridors of the school. A stern disciplinarian, and remorseless pursuer of malefactors, he gave weekly addresses in assembly, remonstrating with us about our patriotic duty, which was to refrain from sabotaging the war effort by slacking, smoking, declining to disturb the brilliantined perfection of our hair by wearing the school cap, and chatting up the girls from the nearby high school at the bus stop. Jefferies had four sons: one had studied law, another medicine; there was one in the church, and one still at Cambridge. We never knew his real opinion of us – it was usually expressed in tones of blistering contempt – but we were not the stuff such achievement is made of; though we did eventually manage a parson and a handful of schoolteachers on top of the foundation of clerks and mechanics. Oh, and a couple of town councillors, one of whom once fought a general election for the Tories in a solid Labour constituency.

And, of course, Huby.

It was easy enough later to realise the foreboding that must often have gripped our elders during those first years of the war; but whatever fears did possess them either they hid them well or we discounted them. It seemed inconceivable to us that we could possibly lose. Some of us had fathers or brothers away in the forces, which brought it a little nearer home. There were evacuees among us who spoke of destruction rained from the skies, in queer southern accents which we cruelly mocked. And uniforms everywhere, austerity, rationing, the blackout. But either morale remained remarkably high or we were deplorably insensitive.

The blacked-out nights cloaked our after-school activities. What *did* we do during those long dark evenings when no glimmer of light broke the façades of houses, when you could not tell if a shop was open or shut till you'd tried the door and stepped round the heavy entrance curtain, when elderly women walked carefully along by the sparse glow of blinkered torches, armed with hat-pin and pepper for defence against the known enemy or that masquerading as daytime friend? We went to the cinema as often as our funds allowed, acquiring an encyclopedic knowledge of the Hollywood film of the period; but there were hardly any school societies and no youth clubs, except the religion-tainted groups run by the local churches, which we were at pains to avoid. So we must often have been bored and in this boredom we sought and found the excitement of petty crime. But we were never apprehended by anyone vengeful enough to make an example of us and the taint did not spread into adult life. At least, so far as I know. One or two of those adolescent rogues standing where Huby is now would tempt me to hindsight and the smug satisfaction of having seen it coming all those years ago. But Huby was not in our gang.

A core of staff too old for military service held the fort among the comings and goings of men conscripted and released. We moved steadily up the school, some of us making the most of what was offered, others inexorably losing ground as they frittered away the advantage our scholarships had given us in a society preponderantly made up of those fated to leave school at fourteen for a life dominated by hourly wage-rates and the time-clock. A changing awareness of the girls down the road brought vanity, which was expressed by a facsimile of adult smartness, in pressed trousers, polished shoes and slickly parted hair. The greater part of our time was spent in the ordinary pursuits of boyhood; but we sampled experiences such as smoking, gambling and fondling girls in the shelter of long grass or the darkness of ginnels with the curiosity and awakening appetite of anyone growing through one stage of life into another which seems more pleasureful and exciting.

There had been a firewatching duty since early 1940: a master and three senior boys sleeping in school every night – the master in the staff room, the lads on campbeds in an attic in the old building. They were supposed to patrol the grounds during an alert and tackle any fires with stirrup pumps until help arrived. The duty was voluntary, but most of us did it for the novelty of sleeping away from home and being in school but outside the discipline of the timetable. We read and yarned, played cards, had a dartboard until too many wild shots pitted the door with holes and it was taken away from us. Some of us smoked, too; always with an ear cocked for footsteps on the bare steps and a paper ready to waft the incriminating fug out of the window. It was an adventure and our activities, though some in violation of the school rules, were innocent enough. Until I did a duty with Eddie Duncalf.

I became aware in the early hours of the morning that Eddie was not in the room. He was absent for some time. The next day I asked him where he'd been. He grinned.

It turned out – and I was not the only one who knew about it – that Eddie had somehow obtained keys which gave him access to the pantry in the kitchen and the store cupboards there. From them he was helping himself to small amounts of the foodstuffs used for school meals: butter, sugar, cheese, tinned meat – anything, in fact, which was scarce or rationed. I went with him once, but creeping along those dark corridors in the night, expecting at every corner to bump into the master in charge, was too much for my nerves. I could never fathom anyway what Eddie did with the stuff. There was not enough for him to trade on the black market, even if he had the contacts; and I couldn't imagine his mother accepting it without explanation. I could only assume he hid it and concocted treats for himself when he was alone in the house.

He made his last raid on a night when Huby was sharing the duty with us. As Eddie crept from the room and down the stairs, Huby spoke across the distance between our beds.

'He's a fool.'

'What?' I responded drowsily.

'Duncalf. He'll get nabbed one of these times.'

'What d'you mean?'

'Don't make out you don't know.'

I snored gently into the darkness.

But Huby was to be proved right; or partly so. For, although Eddie was not caught in the act, the outcome was the same. The cook had apparently known for some time that pilfering was taking place. This particular week she had taken an extra-careful inventory and when Eddie over-reached himself and stole more than usual she was able to pinpoint the losses with accuracy. There was an enquiry among the kitchen staff. No culprit could be found there. Then a cleaner remembered seeing currants and raisins on the floor of the firewatching room. Heathcote Jefferies questioned the masters first, then summoned to his study all the lads on that week's roster.

We lined up, jostling shoulder to shoulder, in an arc across the front of his desk. Jefferies, at the window, waited till we'd settled before spinning round and reaching for a list of names. He checked us off against this without speaking, then took his stance at one end of the mantelshelf.

'There's been some stealing from the pantry.' His gaze raked across the line of faces. 'The culprit is someone who has been on firewatching duty in the last week.'

No one spoke. Jefferies must already have selected the likelier suspects, for there were among us some members of swots' corner who would no more have robbed the pantry than smoke a cigarette or fail to do their homework diligently. Three of them, Tolson, Lindsay and Carter, did duty together and were standing at one end of the line. Jefferies began with them.

'Did you steal from the pantry?'

'No, sir.'

'Did you steal from the pantry?'

'No, sir.'

'Carter, did you steal from the pantry?'

'No, sir.'

'Did you steal from the pantry?'

'Oh, no, sir.' This was Billy Morrison, a good lad, who knew about Eddie but would never have dreamed of giving him away.

Jefferies paused here and changed his tactics.

'Do any of you boys know who did steal from the pantry?'

This was one of Jefferies's least likeable traits, his inviting you to shop someone else. Morrison spoke for all of us. 'No, sir.' I thought afterwards that it was a trick of the light, but I wanted to believe that his lip did visibly curl and that Jefferies noticed it.

Jefferies returned to the direct question.

'Did you steal from the pantry?'

'No, sir.'

'No, sir.'

'No, sir.'
'No, sir.'
'No, sir.'
Eddie: 'No sir.'
'No, sir.' Me.

A stonewall defence. He couldn't break it. He had come to Huby, who was last in line.

'Did you steal from the pantry, Huby?'

'No, sir.'

We were through.

But Jefferies, stuck with all those monosyllabic denials, let his gaze linger on Huby for another couple of seconds. And Huby, unable to make do with that simple and unbreakable 'no', rushed in and sank the boat.

'I was in the room, sir.'

Jefferies pounced. 'Which room?'

'The firewatching room, sir.'

'How do you know?'

'I don't know what you mean, sir.'

'How do you know you were in the firewatching room?'

'I was, sir.'

'You mean it couldn't have been you who stole from the pantry because you were in the firewatching room at the time?'

'Yes, sir. I mean, no, sir.'

'So, if you didn't do it, it must have been somebody who was on duty with you. Eh?'

'No, sir.'

'But you've just told me that it happened while you were on duty, but it wasn't you because you were in the firewatching room.'

'No, sir.'

'So you weren't in the firewatching room?'

'I was, sir.'

'At the time the pantry was being burgled.'

It was no longer a question but a statement. Huby floundered. He went red. His mouth trembled. He was lost.

'Yes, sir.'

Duncalf came back to the form-room alone twenty minutes later, beaten and angry, and with a threat of expulsion hanging over him which, as it happened, was never carried out. 'You absolute blithering idiot, Huby. If you aren't the most useless sod I've ever met.'

But he wasn't, as he was not many years in showing.

It was working for the press that kept me in touch with Huby's early fortunes and made me aware of him again when he really started to rise into the big time. I ran into him now and then before I moved to a provincial evening paper from the local weekly. He was clerking for an uncle, marking time before he went off to do his National Service. When he came back he began to do small deals in scrap metal and before long he'd branched out into war-surplus materials. He made quite a bit of money, married a girl from the town and moved into a new four-bedroomed house.

Then I lost sight of him until, subbing on a national daily in Fleet Street, I began to see news pars about him and, when his first wife divorced him and he married a girl fifteen years younger than himself, the occasional photograph. By this time he was going up fast; everything he touched seemed to prosper. His interests were widespread: mail order, unit furniture, domestic appliances. I don't know what quality he discovered in himself and nourished so successfully that he became a millionaire by forty, because, frankly, I don't understand that kind of talent.

It was the business editor who ran through the list of Huby's interests for me and who later, aware now that I'd known him once, warned me of the whispers which preceded the investigation into his affairs and the eventual bringing of charges. Facing the music with him are a couple of fellow directors and the secretary of one of his companies. I don't know, of course, whether Huby is guilty or not, whether his substance is solid or just a bubble blown by him or his colleagues. But a number of offences do seem to have been committed and it looks as though the real issue is who is going to carry the can.

What I'm wondering now is whether Mr Heathcote Jefferies Jr, QC, who is to open for the Crown, is as good an interrogator as his father was, seizing on any tiny slip to force, with the ruthless sharpness of his mind and the overwhelming power of his personality, a breach in a solid wall of falsehood. Does he know that Huby was one of his father's pupils years ago?

Probably not, and it doesn't matter. The old man had no doubt forgotten the incident long before he died.

But I know what I'd be feeling if I were in the dock with Huby tomorrow, aware that the penalty this time will not be six of the best but more like a year or two inside and a paralysing fine. And waiting – oh, the sweaty palmed, stomach-fluttering waiting – for Huby to be offered and succumb to that fatal temptation to enlarge.

Good

Caroline rang again that morning, at a quarter to nine, after Fred had left the house but before peak rate started. Jean accepted the transfer-charge call.

'Mum. Sorry about that, but I'm short of change.'

'That's all right, love. You must never let that stop you.' Jean put a smile into her voice. 'Mind you, your father *did* have a word or two to say about our conversation ten days ago. It was on the bill that came yesterday. Nearly four pounds' worth.'

'Oh, dear! Did you tell him what we were talking about?'

'No, I didn't. Time enough for that, if – ' She stopped herself. 'What news have you got?'

'None, really.'

'You mean there's no change?'

'Hmm.'

'How's Alan?'

'Well . . . fretting a bit.'

'I expect he is. But from what you told me . . .'

'Oh yes. All the same, it's worrying.'

'This thing is going to be a worry in years to come as well, unless someone can do something about it. Have you seen a doctor or do you want to wait till you come home?'

'It could be too late then.'

'Don't be silly. I didn't mean that. I'm sure it's nothing now.'

'I've made an appointment here. I'm going tomorrow.'

Jean's younger daughter had irregular periods, a minor nuisance until she met a boy at university and began to sleep with him. Sleep with him! Ye Gods! What Jean's mother would have said to *her*! What Caroline's father would say if her education was put at risk. Not that it *would* come to that, but Jean did wish that Caroline was where they could talk face to face, taking as long as they needed, and not nearly two hundred miles away on the end of a telephone. Thank goodness, though, the child felt able to share her worry. She had always told all three of them – they both had, come to that – that if anything was wrong they should come to them first. *Anything*, she had said. Because even the nicest, best adjusted of children had to live in the same world as everyone else.

Stephen was still in bed. When she had finished her chat with Caroline, Jean took him up a cup of tea. He had shown no desire to go to university and so had not screwed himself to that extra pitch of effort to qualify for entrance. Now Jean rather suspected he wished he had: the three extra years of study would have kept him off the labour market. He did not know what he wanted to do. In better times he could have taken any old job until he found his path. But the better times had slipped into economic recession and there were no jobs; all he had now was this morale-sapping life on the dole. Fred said he had a school full of younger Stephens. 'What can I tell them?' he would say. 'How can I spur them on when I know full well that most of them are destined for the scrapheap at eighteen? Some of these kids may never work. I can't see who*ever*'s in power getting three and a half million back into jobs. We shall reap the whirlwind of all this in ten or fifteen years' time,' he would brood at his most pessimistic, 'with an alienated generation that won't be integrated into a society that's shown such little regard for them.'

Stephen stirred under his duvet as she went into the room and spoke to him. She put the teacup on his bedside table and told him not to let it go cold. He had always been sluggish in the mornings. Jean had sympathised with all three of them in the amount of sleep they needed while they were growing. But this lying late in bed every day was not right for a young man of Stephen's age. Yet how could she blame him? What challenge did the days hold to get him up each morning? The world was wasting him.

'If you want me to cook breakfast for you, you'd better not
be long because I've got to go out.'

'I'll see to it myself.'

'There are eggs and bacon and sausages in the fridge.'

'Naw. Mebbe I'll have them at lunchtime.'

As his head emerged, she noted again that he badly needed a
shave. But she did not put that down to his present lethargy: an
incipient beard seemed to be a mark of his age group.

'What will you do today?'

'Dunno.'

'You could start by cleaning this place up. It's like a tip.'

'Oh, Mum . . .'

Yes, Oh Mum. Afraid now of nagging, Jean mostly let
things slide, thereby abetting him in his apathy. During the last
depression, in the thirties, proud men had polished their worn
shoes, snipped threads from fraying cuffs and collars and gone
out each morning to haunt labour exchanges and factory gates,
then shop-window gaze or linger in the reading-rooms of
public libraries until it was time to go home and pretend for
another day that they were still employed. Until what savings
they had ran out and they had to face their families and own
up.

Jean's mother had told her things like that. The bad times for
her had had back luck thrown in for good measure. Widowed
when Jean and her brother were still young, she had turned her
hand to any mortal thing that was legal and decent to bring
them up and put them through grammar school. Jean's stan-
dards of fortitude had been set by her mother's example. You
held on, never let go, worked till you could hardly stand, asked
for nothing that was not your due and fought tooth and nail for
everything that was. 'You know all about poverty,' Jean could
hear her saying, 'but I'll see you're never familiar with
squalor.' But that extra two years at grammar school – four
earning years between her and Jack – had been the limit of what
could be managed. No college or university for them. Jack
might have become a civil servant, instead of settling for local
government; she herself would surely have become a teacher;
probably out of the house again and doing something interesting ever since the children had stopped needing constant care
and attention. But that had become her role, the purpose of her

life: to look after Fred and the kids, make a good home for them, see that they had everything she could provide.

Had she done it well? She could only measure that against the failure she saw every day: surly, disaffected children; husbands and wives with hardly a good word for each other; others leading their own, separate lives, drifted apart, some of them split up. *She* had been lucky: the two who were away kept in touch, came home; all three confided. There had been that terrible time, quite early on, when Fred had become infatuated with that unmarried teacher from the school in Calderford. 'I can have a friendship, can't I?' he had pleaded, when even she had seen what couldn't be hidden any longer. And for months she had sweated through nights when he didn't touch her and others when he clung wordlessly to her, making love in a silent frenzy, as if to drive the demon of infidelity out of himself.

And they were still together. It was never spoken of, never brought up, thrown out. Yes, she had done it well and she had been lucky. All the same, there were times when . . . But never mind.

Stephen had not come down by the time she had drunk another cup of tea herself and washed up her and Fred's breakfast pots. She put on her coat, took her shopping bags and called from the foot of the stairs: 'I'm taking my key in case you want to go out. Make sure you lock the door and I'll see you for lunch.' She waited. 'Do you hear?'

She backed the car carefully into the street. She had the use of it during the day now that Fred, with a doleful recognition of his thickening waist, had taken to cycling the two miles to school. This was one of those mornings when she was glad not to have to wait for a bus: blustery, whipping the poplars of the garden opposite, with rain in the wind. Straightening the vehicle, she fastened her seatbelt, managed that stiff initial push into bottom gear and drove off to her first call.

'Was that your car making all that noise?' Mollie Tyler asked, handing Jean her cup of coffee.

'I'm afraid the exhaust's gone. I heard it rasping a bit the other day but I quite forgot to ask Fred or Stephen to look underneath. It's nearly four years old. Stephen gets on to Fred regularly about part-exchanging it while he can still get a decent price. But Fred's having one of his periodic economy drives.'

'Oh?'

'I don't mean he's penny-pinching. But I know he'd like us to see Venice this year and he does feel the burden of Caroline's fees and having to subsidise Stephen. I mean, he's got to let the lad keep most of his dole if he's to have any life at all.'

'Oh yes, you've got to give them their chance.'

'Well, Caroline, anyway. All Stephen can hope for at present is that things will pick up before all the stuffing's knocked out of him.'

Mollie's two daughters were living away, married to men with good prospects. Mollie herself, widowed twelve months ago, was only just recovering from having a breast removed.

'But how are you feeling?' Jean asked.

'Oh, pretty fair. I think they're just about ready to give me a clean bill of health.'

'Oh, that *is* good news, Mollie.'

'Yes, it could all have been a lot worse.'

'Is that a new dress?'

'Yes. I thought I'd treat myself.' Standing, Mollie drew herself up in the closely fitting tweed frock. 'You couldn't tell, could you?'

'You'd have no idea. You look as good as ever.'

'Yes, I look all there,' Mollie said wryly, 'even if I know I'm not.'

Jean had always admired Mollie's figure and envied her ability to keep it trim yet shapely without the fussy regimen that so many women had to adopt. In her late forties, she was a woman with looks enough to choose her way into a good second marriage, if ever she wanted one. But what now? Jean wondered. At what stage did you tell a man that what he saw and liked was not all it seemed? And what were the chances of being doubly lucky and picking a man you really wanted who would also swallow his disappointment and accept it as part of the bargain?

'I've got a bit of shopping to do. I wondered if there was anything you wanted.'

'I'm all right, Jean. I can manage all that.'

'Well, you look fit enough just now, but you didn't sound it on the phone the other day.'

'Oh, that was just this bug that's going around. You're sick and on the run for twenty-four hours and then it leaves you. Have you managed to keep clear of it?'

'Well, so far, yes. There's been a bit of it among the staff at Fred's school.'

'He's all right, is he, Fred?'

'Yes, he's fine.'

'And how's Caroline? Still enjoying herself.'

'Oh, yes. She's settled to it nicely.'

'When are we going to talk about that coffee morning?'

'There's the flag day before then.'

'Yes, well, we ought to give people plenty of time, so's they've no excuses. Otherwise it'll be the same old story: leave it to Jean; she'll see that it's all right.'

'They usually rally round, when it comes to it.'

'Some do, some don't.'

'Don't make me out to be a martyr, Mollie.'

'That's your word, not mine. Whenever have I heard you moan?'

'What have I got to moan about?'

'There's not one of us who hasn't got something, at some time or other.' She looked up as Jean sighed. 'That came from deep down. Was it for something special?'

'I was just thinking that you shame me, Mollie. With all that's happened to you, what right have I to grumble?'

'If you've got something to grumble about, grumble.'

'That's just the point. I haven't.'

All the same . . .

The woman came back into the greengrocer's as Jean was transferring her purchases from the counter to her shopping bag.

'I'm just wondering if you've given me the right change . . .'

Jean only half heard as she lingered, thinking there was something else she needed. The customer went again. 'Sorry, my mistake.'

The woman behind the counter took coins from the still-open till and handed them to Jean. 'There's *your* change, dear. Thirty-seven pence.'

Jean was outside before it clicked in her mind. Opening her purse, she checked the coins in there, then took those the woman had given her from her pocket. She went back in and to the head of the queue.

'Excuse me.'

'Yes, love.' The woman glanced up from her rapid serving.

'My change.'

'It must be catching today,' the woman said. 'I did give it to you, you know, love. What was it, now? Thirty-seven pence.'

'Yes, but you've given it to me twice. I know by the coins in my purse. I hadn't that much loose change when I came in.' She handed the money back.

'Well, thank you.' The woman smiled. 'I must have been dreaming.'

'Both of us, come to that,' Jean said.

'Aye, well, I don't know about you, love,' the woman said, 'but it's not dinnertime yet, and I could lose a small fortune by half-past five.' She put her head back, her fleshy throat above the neck of a shocking-pink jumper pumping uninhibited laughter out of her broad chest.

Mrs Rawdon stopped Jean as she reached the pavement on the other side of the street. Preoccupied, Jean would have walked past her.

'Mrs Nesbit.' She was a small deferential body in a worn tweed coat.

'I'm sorry. I hadn't seen you.'

'Oh, you've more to think about than me.'

Jean looked into the pale crumpled face and wondered, as she had before, how anyone without an ailment could nowadays age so much before her time.

'How is your husband, Mrs Rawdon?'

'That's why I stopped you.' The woman shook her head. 'I'm afraid . . .'

'I'm sorry.'

'We cremated him the day before yesterday.'

'Had he been in hospital?'

'Oh, yes. They had to take him back in the end. I'm glad I've seen you, though. I thought you ought to know, you having been so kind to us.'

'It was nothing,' Jean said. 'I happened to know about the Trust, that's all.'

'It made all the difference, though, having that holiday. We both enjoyed it. It seemed . . . well, it seemed to bring us together again.'

'I'm glad. Are *you* all right now?'

'Oh, I shall manage, don't you fear.'

'Good.'

Jean had pleaded the woman's need for a break, more than her husband's. Should she, she had asked, be penalised for her loyalty to a man who had spent all on drink and gambling? They did like nice comfortable cases of hardship, these guardians of ancient funds, where all concerned were equally deserving.

'Are you all right yourself, Mrs Nesbit, if you don't mind me asking?'

'Yes, of course.' Mrs Rawdon was peering solicitously into her face. 'Why?' she found herself adding.

'Just my feeling. I saw you as you crossed over the road, and wondered.'

'I was miles away.'

'Yes. I expect you can always find plenty to think about.'

'It seems to find *me*, Mrs Rawdon.'

Surprising Jean considerably, Mrs Rawdon said, 'In an empty mind there's room for nothing. But you can always cram a bit more into a full one. But excuse me. I've delayed you long enough.'

It was on the tip of Jean's tongue to say, 'Let me know if I can be of any help,' but she held it back and let the woman go, not knowing whether she might be asked later for something she could not give. One had to be practical about these things.

Was she all right? Of course she was all right.

It was as she was scoffing at Mrs Rawdon's curious fancy that the feeling came upon her. She could not have told anyone what it actually felt *like*. There was no sense of faintness or physical fatigue, but quite suddenly she realised that she could not make up her mind what to do next. Aware that she had not moved from where Mrs Rawdon had left her, she looked in through the big windows of the supermarket, saw the queues at the checkouts and knew that she could not go in. It was silly. The crush was unusual and would soon clear. There were things she needed, things she had left the house to buy. But she did not want to enter the place. The thought of doing so aroused in her something like panic.

She felt sweat break out on her neck and forehead. Well, at her age, she knew what her doctor or her friends would make of that. And yet, there was something more. What the devil was it all about? What was it all for? If she bought groceries now they would get eaten and she would have to come back for more. As when she cleaned the house or weeded the garden. The house got dirty again; more weeds grew. So it went on. Nothing was ever settled. You ate to live, to eat to live, to eat . . . Brought up a new generation to do the same. And what was ever *accomplished*?

Forcing her legs to work, she turned and went slowly along the parade of shops: jewellery and watches, shoes, meat, an optician's, magazines and newspapers . . . There was another supermarket, recently opened, round the corner. People she knew had shopped there. She had told herself she would try it some time and compare its range of goods and prices. She quickened her pace slightly, turning her head once as, after several seconds' delay, she fancied someone had given her a greeting.

The premises of the new store were not a conversion but entirely new, of raw red brick, built on the site of a demolished building. Jean entered, took a wire basket from a pile and went through the barrier. The layout of the shelves was strange. She looked at the hanging notices which offered general guidance and consulted the slip of paper on which she had made her list.

Special offers, new lines, loss leaders. So many pence off this and that, but be careful because now you were in here with everything to hand you could lose that advantage by paying over the odds for something else. She wandered, her mind still drifting, refusing to focus, while she picked things up, looked, put some things back, put others into the basket. She was buying more than she had come for. It was hard not to do that in a new place, with fresh brands, different labels. All set out to hand, so that you didn't have to ask. All set out to tempt you to second and third thoughts. Help yourself. Take what you want and pay for it. Or don't pay. Defray the rising cost of living by stealing a proportion of your weekly shopping list. They did it – some did, she didn't know who they were – and got away with it. Some did. They must, or there would not be those occasional reports of the percentages these big concerns wrote off. And it must be easy, so easy, to drop one thing into the store's basket and another into the open mouth of your own bag. To think that there must be people who came out every shopping day with that intention. Or was it more casual than that, more haphazard, tempted suddenly and taking a chance?

Jean was through the checkout and on the pavement outside before she felt the hand on her elbow and heard the voice that froze her to the spot.

'Excuse me, madam, but haven't you got something in your bag that you haven't paid for?'

Turning her head, forcing herself to look into the woman's expressionless face.

'I think you've made a mistake.'

'If I have, perhaps we can sort it out in private, inside.'

The hand tightened its grip slightly. Jean wondered what would happen if she refused, shook herself free, made off. People were looking. The beat of her heart was sickening. Was this how it always went? she wondered. Why couldn't the woman see that this was special, different?

The manager's office, a tiny room with a yellow wood desk, a filing cabinet and two chairs, was at the back of the store. The woman let Jean walk to it in front of her. The manager was a young man with sandy hair and an absurd little moustache. It was perhaps his first important appointment. He asked Jean's name. She told him. He wrote it down.

'What's the address?'

'Thirty-three Willow Grove.'

'Is that nearby?'

'Three or four minutes by car.'

'Have you shopped here before?'

'I usually go to Dunstan's.'

'But you thought we'd be easier to steal from?'

'This is all a mistake.'

'Mrs Nesbit, we have TV surveillance here, with instant playback. Right? Would you like us to show you what we saw?'

Jean said nothing. No, she would not like that.

They emptied the contents of her bags on to the desk top, separated the goods she had bought elsewhere and checked the rest against her till-slip. The manager sighed then lifted the telephone and dialled a number.

'Will you send somebody round as soon as possible.' He listened. 'Yes. Yes.'

'If I've got something I didn't pay for it's because I didn't know I had it,' Jean said.

'Whether you took it deliberately or not will be for the court to decide. Right?'

'You mean you actually intend to prosecute?'

'It's company policy. Out of my hands. We always prosecute. We're new here. One or two convictions to start with might stop it getting a hold. Right?'

'But over a little thing like that.'

'Little or big makes no difference.'

'Do you seriously think I'd risk my reputation for such a trivial thing?'

'I don't know about your reputation. For all I know, you might make a habit of it.'

'I've never done such a thing in my life before,' Jean said, adding quickly, 'I haven't done anything now.'

'I don't know why you don't just own up,' the manager said.

The woman who had apprehended Jean, youngish, straw-coloured hair cut short, was silent, standing with her back to the filing cabinet. Her glance kept lifting above Jean's head. Jean looked round. In the corner on the wall a closed circuit television screen flickered silently. She saw shoppers among the banks of shelves. 'I'd advise you to change your tune when you get into court,' the manager was saying. 'They don't like to have their time wasted. You can always plead a mental blackout. That's a steady favourite.' His voice was edged with sarcasm. Jean felt herself colouring afresh.

The police constable was young too, though with dark hair and a soft complexion. He glanced at Jean when he came in and looked round as though expecting to see someone else. He was visibly embarrassed as the manager spoke to him and held up the tin of pilchards.

'Is this it?'

'That's it.'

'Nothing else?'

'Isn't it enough?'

'You're sure there's no mistake?'

'Whose side are you on?' the manager asked.

The young constable bristled. 'There's no need for that, sir. It's just that I know this lady, and –'

'You know her, you say?'

'Well, not personally.' He looked at Jean. 'Your husband taught me at school.'

The manager pointed to the television screen. 'Look, I've spent enough time with this. Right? See for yourself.' He pressed switches.

Jean found herself wondering how long they kept tapes like that; if it would be destroyed when it had served its immediate purpose or kept on file to condemn her forever.

She got Fred on his own after their evening meal, when Stephen had left the house for some vague rendezvous.

'Fred, there's something I've got to tell you.'

'Yes?'

'Put the paper down. It's very important.'

'All right. I'm listening.'

'The police might come.'

'Here?'

'Yes.'

'Whatever for? Is Stephen in trouble?'

'No, it's me.'

'Have you clouted the car?'

'No.' Jean drew a deep breath. 'I'm being prosecuted for shoplifting.'

'You're *what*?'

'I took something from that new supermarket in Cross Street this morning. They called me back inside and sent for the police.'

'You're pulling my leg.'

'I'm not, Fred.'

'But . . . What did you take? Did you really take it?'

'A tin of pilchards. I really did take it.'

He was incredulous. 'A tin of pilchards! You mean to tell me they called in the police over a tin of pilchards?'

'They said it was company policy always to prosecute.'

'My God!' He was speechless for some time. Jean poured herself another cup of coffee. 'You personally know half the Bench,' Fred said, lifting his hand in a gesture of refusal as she held the coffee pot over his cup. She was surprised at the steadiness of her hand.

'The ones who know me will have to stand down, I expect.'

'Will it really come to that?'

'They said so. They said they had to make an example of anyone they caught.'

'They'll let you off.'

'No, I'm afraid not.'

'The Bench, I mean. You're well known in the town. You're a person of . . . of standing.'

'All the worse, I suppose. I should know better. And it's not as if I were in need.'

'Of a tin of pilchards? Who needs a tin of pilchards? What made you take a tin of *pilchards*?'

'I saw them on the shelf and remembered that Stephen is fond of them.'

'Pilchards? Stephen likes pilchards? Buy him some, then. Buy a dozen tins and keep them in the cupboard.' He stopped, then looked straight at her. 'You're not ill, are you?'

'No. I don't think so.' She had not thought of that. No, that wasn't it. She must not let them make her out to be ill.

'You'll have to deny it. They'll believe you. They'll have to believe it's a mistake.'

'I've no defence, Fred. They have a television tape.'

'Christ! This is going to look fine in the *Argus*. And don't think the *Evening Post* won't pick it up as well.' He strained his neck out of his shirt, then loosened his tie. He needed a bigger collar size; she had noticed that before. 'How is it going to affect *my* position? I'm always having to chastise light-fingered kids. I can see their smirks now. They'll make a meal of it. They'll have me for breakfast, dinner and tea.'

He got up and went to the cupboard where they kept their small stock of drink. He took out the whisky bottle. 'Do you want one?'

'No, thanks.' She wondered when she would start crying.

He poured one for himself, then said, 'I'm sorry if I seem selfish; thinking about myself. But I'm trying to imagine all the consequences.'

'I'm not blaming you, Fred. After all, you didn't do it. I did.'

'Yes, and I still can't understand. I can't for the life of me understand what could have possessed you.'

'It was a feeling that came over me. That's the only way I can explain it.'

'What kind of feeling?' But she merely shrugged. 'You're not some crack-brained neurotic housewife trying to make up her bingo losses, or somebody who steals for kicks. You know better. You're as honest as the day's long. You're sturdy, dependable. People know you, respect you, look up to you.'

'A good woman,' Jean murmured.

'What?' Then he caught it. 'Yes – *good*.'

'Yes, I'm good,' she wanted to say to him. 'I *am* good. But how can I prove how good I *am*, unless I do something bad?'

She wanted to say it, but she didn't. She did not think he would understand that.

The Apples of Paradise

It was a dazzling morning. Though patches of frost still lay white in shadowed corners, the big winds of the past week had gone and it was possible with the warmth of the sun on one's shoulders to stand without feeling chilled.

Hare had slipped into a rear pew of the chapel just before the coffin entered and now he took a place on the asphalt path, a little way from the family group round the open grave and separated again from the cluster of invited guests who would be returning to the house for refreshment.

Chapel and graveyard stood high on a hill. Wholesale demolition of old property had opened up a fresh view of the town and a wide green sweep of cropped grass bordering a new road had left the once closed-in Victorian building in a rather striking isolation. This had been a town of non-conformist churches in Hare's youth. Now the few left struggled on with amalgamated congregations, their one-time differences in Methodist doctrine submerged in their need to survive.

Hare felt one or two glances of half-recognition as the parson intoned, but Fell himself had his back to him and the two women whom Hare took to be Tom's daughters, stand-ing arm in arm with their men, had been too young when he left the town to know now who he was.

Waiting, Hare assumed his demeanour to be one of sombre composure, but his stomach felt empty and faintly nauseous and he was not sure how he would react to Fell's quite proper and expected display of grief. Hare didn't think he could cope with Tom's tears, and Tom had never been afraid to cry when given cause.

Hare was perturbed by a sudden thickening in his throat. And they were finished. He must control himself. He stepped forward as Fell turned and walked towards him.

'Tom . . .'

Fell stopped and peered into his face. 'Gerald? You came, Gerald.'

Fell took Hare's gloved hand between both of his and they examined each other. The changes in the look of a friend one sees regularly are almost as imperceptible as those observed in one's own looking-glass, but these two had been apart and nearly thirty years masked for each the youthful face he'd known and kept as the only possible memory.

'You're looking very well, Gerald.'

And Tom, Hare thought, seemed uncharacteristically stoic in his self-possession.

Fell's daughters hovered for a moment, then proceeded slowly to the gate and the waiting car.

'I'm sorry, Tom,' Hare said. 'I truly am.'

Fell shook his head and looked at the ground. 'A bad do, Gerald. A bad do. We could have had another ten or fifteen year. But,' he glanced into Hare's face now with a regretful little smile, 'it wasn't meant to be.'

Hare was the taller of the two. His weight had increased no more than a few pounds since his twenties and, apart from a small round pot-belly, hardly noticeable under his well-cut clothes, he was as lean and trim as then. His smooth dark hair showed a powdering of grey, with two white wings above his ears. Fell had always been the stocky one and now he was comfortably round, though, still, Hare had noticed, light on his small feet. A few strands of once fair-to-gingerish hair were combed across the totally bald crown of his round head.

'But come back home, Gerald, where we can talk in the warm. Have you got a car?'

'Yes, it's just down the road. But I can't, Tom.'

'You're not going back straight away?'

'No, but there's something else I must see to.'

Hare had not planned this refusal. It was just that now, watching the people leave the graveyard, he felt a sudden violent wish not to have to talk to anybody else and, as a focus of reminiscence, become a welcome diversion in the uneasy aftermath of the funeral.

'Will you be at home tomorrow?'

'Oh, aye.'

'What if I came round then?'

'Yes,' Fell said, 'come round when we can be quiet and on our own.' They settled on a time. 'You know where it is, of course?' Fell said with a flicker of humour.

'I think I can still find it,' Hare replied.

Hare could hardly remember a time when he didn't know Fell; certainly, he could not recall how they had met. It must have been at Sunday school. Both Hare's family and Fell's had been Methodist and rigidly insistent on the boys' attendance at chapel three times every Sunday. Fell's father was an iron-monger; Hare's had owned, in partnership, a furniture shop. Much of the furniture Hare's father had sold was made on the premises by three craftsmen. It had a name for quality. Their steel-framed three-piece suites were said to last a lifetime, and in those inter-war years long before the coming of discount warehouses of the type Hare himself had ended up owning, when their main rivals were the cheapjack city shops who attracted a different kind of customer anyway, their reputation spread miles beyond the boundaries of the little town.

Approaching their teens, both Hare and Fell were enrolled as fee-paying pupils at a grammar school; not the local one to which they could have won free places through County Minor Scholarships, but an older foundation in the nearby city with a better academic record. Fell was a year younger than Hare and in a lower form; but they continued together at chapel where at one period, in their early teens, they pumped the organ together for morning and evening services. It was felt to be a job for two lads as the pipes were not as sound as they might have been and keeping them filled with air called for consider-able exertion. The one time Hare did it alone found him at the end of the service exhausted, his skin bathed in sweat and his heart pounding. It was unfortunate that Fell's absence had coincided with that of the regular organist and the appearance of a deputy notorious for the pace at which he dragged out hymns, as well as his seizing a chance of practice by launching on an extended voluntary as the congregation filed out. But Hare liked the duty because it allowed him and Fell, tucked away behind their screen, seclusion from the people in the body of the chapel during the services, with whose content he was becoming bored and disillusioned.

It was at about the time Hare was privately rejecting its teachings that the chapel played host to a two-week evangelical mission of students from a Methodist college who were being trained for the ministry. The mission culminated in 'conversions', when the erring, the strayed and the sore-at-heart were enjoined to come forward to the communion rail, there to kneel and be born again in Christ: to be 'saved'.

Hare sat through it with a mounting discomfort of spirit. It wasn't merely the small-minded rigidity that characterised many of the chapel's regulars which more and more alienated him. There were to him too many flaws in the gospel preached from that pulpit week after week: too many anomalies that his intellect could not accept and which his faith was not strong enough to overlook. He realised that, more than simply rejecting the teaching of his church, he was beginning to doubt the existence of God in any form he found acceptable. He had never discussed this with Fell or anyone else and when, to his mild surprise, Fell got up and went forward to kneel with the others at the rail, Hare decided to keep his own counsel until such time as he could reach a clear decision. That, he felt, would be when his reluctance to displease his parents was outweighed by distaste for his lip-service. In any case, war threatened. Chamberlain had averted one crisis, but Hitler was making more and more demands. A war would change a lot of things.

Fell started courting a cheerful fresh-faced girl from among those who had pledged themselves to the Lord during the mission. Hare decided that Fell's conversion had been less for its own sake than a way of making himself more acceptable, of showing himself to be serious, to Emily Schofield. In later years Hare could blame his inability to reconcile Laura Sherwood's chapel-going with his own hardening doubt for his failure to make sure of her when she seemed to welcome his attentions. Laura was neatly shod. Her hair was tucked under a little blue hat. The collar of a white blouse encircled her slim throat. The soft stuff of the blouse formed a V between the lapels of her plainly tailored costume-coat. The coat hinted at a gentle fullness of breast that stirred Hare to a tenderness which lodged under his heart in a weight of longing.

When he first saw her he did not know who she was; knew nothing about her except that she had emerged, bible in hand, from the nearest of the town's other Methodist chapels. A few days later she came into the shop while he was waiting on counter. She had a couple of chairs which needed re-covering: would he show her some material and give her a price? Hare said he would call himself. She gave him her name and her address: The Cottage, Millbank Lane. He told her that he had seen her coming out of her chapel and she said she had chosen it because it seemed most like the one she had attended before they moved to the town. No, she had not been here long; less than a year. Her father had retired early from his business because of ill-health. He was a widower and she kept house for him.

There was about her a haunting womanliness, a gentleness and a natural grace which made the other girls he knew look either cheap or gawky and his thoughts seem shameful. He felt she would have been profoundly shocked to know of some of the things which flitted through his mind. He knew little of these matters and during the walks they began to take together in the long summer evenings of those months just before the war he avoided physical contact and any familiarity of speech. He did not know what she expected of him and was terrified of offending her. When war was declared, knowing that he would eventually be conscripted, Hare volunteered for the RAF and flying duties. 'I shall pray for you,' Laura told him.

He was sent for training to Canada and came back as a navigator to a squadron of Coastal Command on operational duty in the Middle East. It was when he had completed his overseas tour and was given a home posting that he met Cynthia. She was all that Laura was not: direct, pleasure-loving, passionate in her seizing of the moment. 'Life's short,' she reminded him as she took him into her bed. 'There's a war on.' It was his late initiation and he was grateful to her. She stripped him of his inhibitions and thoughts of her sustained him during the long patrols over the Atlantic. Periods of hazardous duty were punctuated by evenings of drinking and heightened gaiety and snatched opportunities of making love. Cynthia helped her father to run his hotel and sometimes she could entertain Hare in her room without fear of scandal.

He counted himself fortunate that he wasn't an infantryman slogging through the desert, or a member of the crew of one of those ships they watched over, heaving below on the ocean with no sight of home or a woman for weeks or months at a time. What Cynthia gave Hare became as necessary to him as a drug. For by this time he was losing his nerve. He thought his luck was bound to run out and he expected every patrol to be his last. The knowledge that he was at much less risk than Bomber Command crews operating over Europe was little consolation. Fear had seized him and wouldn't let go. They married by special licence. When he awoke sweating in the night as his aircraft plunged towards the grey swell of sea, Cynthia was there to be clung to.

Hare brought his wife home to an empty house. His father had died of a heart attack while Hare was overseas and his mother decided to go and live near Hare's sister, who had already married and moved away before the war. The speed with which the rift between himself and Cynthia opened surprised Hare. Peacetime marriage to a shopkeeper was different from a wartime one to an officer of RAF Coastal Command. She found it dull. It bored her. There was no sign of her conceiving and starting a family and she soon grew restless. Her manner took on a bitter edge, as though she felt she had been deceived. She had the house refurnished and still disliked it. She persuaded Hare to acquire a plot of land and start to build a new house. He also bought a flat at Scarborough, where she spent more and more time. She became friendly with a set there who hung around a hotel bar at weekends and drank cocktails. Hare found them brittle, living on their nerves, and left Cynthia to it.

Tom Fell had waited for call-up, failed the medical and been excused military service. He married Emily Schofield and, by the time Hare was demobbed, was the father of two girls. When the first post-war elections were held he stood for the Urban District Council and took his seat as an independent, benefiting from the belief of many working people in the town that while you might vote Labour in parliamentary elections, in local ones you were wise to choose men of substance who would look after the town's money while looking after their own. It was an argument whose logic made Hare smile; but when more seats became vacant he was persuaded by Fell to stand on the same platform. They were both important and respected men in the town, Fell argued, and it was right that they should have a say in what looked like being its new prosperity. They were, in any case, the kind of men who could attend council meetings held during working hours and it was their responsibility to guide the community's affairs.

'I hear you're building a house,' Fell remarked one day as they stood alone together at the window of the council chamber, before a meeting.

'It's Cynthia's idea,' Hare said. 'I'm happy enough with the old one.'

'I'll be glad of first refusal when you come to sell.'

'I'll remember.'

'Putting up something with a bit of style?'

'It'll be big enough, anyway.'

'Two or three kids,' Fell hinted. 'They'll soon fill it for you.'

'Nay,' Hare said, 'there doesn't seem to be much prospect of that.'

'I'm sorry to hear that, Gerald. My two lasses are a great joy.'

'We shall rattle round it like two peas in a drum,' Hare said gloomily. And, he added to himself, with as much likelihood of touching.

Where had all that gone to, he wondered, all that passion? How could Cynthia have lost interest to the point where pride stopped him from pressing himself on her? She behaved towards him now as though he had cheated her, as if he had promised her something he'd known he could never fulfil. He had even begun to harbour fears for her mental stability.

'She doesn't seem to want to mix much,' Fell was saying.

'Who, Cynthia?'

'Yes. Emily thought she perhaps ought to call and see her, but she doesn't want to push herself.'

It was an idea. There were activities Cynthia could share in, charities she could help support. People here tended not to make a fuss; they left you to yourself until you showed that that was not your choice.

'We don't see you at chapel, Gerald,' Fell said.

'No. Cynthia's not a chapel-goer, and neither am I any longer.'

'That seems a pity.'

Hare didn't choose to discuss with Fell his loss of faith, but now he said, 'I wish Emily would call. Perhaps Cynthia's felt out of place, plumped down here in a town where everybody's known everybody since Adam was a lad.'

The chamber was filling, the chairman of the council about to call for order. 'Put her up to it,' Hare said. 'See what happens.'

He saw Laura Sherwood at a distance in the street and stepped into a shop as she walked towards him. There had been nothing spoken between them to account for the embarrass-ment he felt. They had corresponded spasmodically at the beginning of the war, but only on the level of news, hers from home, his, censored, from the other side of the world. She had been away during the leave given him between his training and his overseas posting, and when her letters stopped he told himself that they had either failed to find him or she had, more likely, formed some attachment. He had not seen or heard of her since his return: it was possible even in a small town to go for long periods without bumping into someone. Now a discreet enquiry told him that she was still unmarried.

She began to fill his thoughts, until he faced himself squarely and acknowledged the bitter mistake he had made. If only he had waited. If only he had kept up their correspondence and used that to begin the courtship he had been too diffident to press while they were together.

It was in the grip of this renewed longing and in the thought that only she stood in his way that his attitude towards Cynthia began to match hers towards him. She seemed surprised that he had turned and, as though excited by the smell of battle, began to provoke open rows.

'How can a man change so much?' she said. 'That's what surprises me.'

'I don't know what you expected. You've got a good living in a comfortable house, in a pleasant town full of pleasant people.'

'That lot, looking at you sideways if you wear anything a bit out of the ordinary. That lot with their bibles under their arms, sticking their tupp'ny-ha'penny noses in the air.'

'You won't try to understand them. You never make one move to be friendly.'

'No, because they bore me rigid; and now you're back among them you're just the same. What happened to that knight of the air in his beautiful blue uniform, that's what I want to know?'

The way she could mock, her head back, dark eyes glittering with malice.

'He was something got up for the duration.'

'Well, I preferred him, even if he was shit-scared half the time.'

Hare flinched and coloured. He could never match the sheer wantonness of her tongue. 'You're fit for nothing but the bar of some pub,' he said, 'swapping dirt with your customers and taking whichever of 'em you fancy into your bed.'

'And what kind of satisfaction do you think you give a woman in bed?'

'It was all some kind of pretence, then, was it, all that at the beginning?'

Her chin came down. The blaze subsided. She seemed genuinely lost herself.

'I don't know what it was,' she muttered, 'except that I must have been out of my mind.'

Suddenly he found hope kindled that she would leave him.

'You'd better decide what you're going to do, then,' he said.

'Do? Do? What is there to do?'

'Clear out. Do what you like. We'll get a divorce.'

'On what grounds?' He saw the spirit flare in her again as she looked at him. 'It'll cost you a packet to get rid of me, Gerald. And that's on top of the scandal.'

He wondered if there was anybody in the Scarborough set with whom she went too far; if her behaviour there could give him a lever. Perhaps he ought to hire someone to watch her. He shrank from the thought.

Hare saw Laura again and this time did not avoid her. She looked at him directly, with a genuine friendliness that seemed free of resentment. He asked after her father.

'I'm afraid he's failing,' she told him. 'He doesn't go out any more.'

'You never come into the shop,' he said. 'You've become quite a stranger.'

'Circumstances change. And you don't buy furniture every other week.'

'True enough.'

'How is your new house progressing?'

'You've heard about that?'

'I saw the builders and someone mentioned your name.'

'It's my wife's idea.'

'How is Mrs Hare? I never see her about the town. Is she well?'

'Oh, she's all right in herself.' He found himself hoping she would detect the lack of concern in his voice.

The weight under his heart seemed to bow his shoulders as he watched her go.

He was standing outside Fell's new double-fronted shop and now the door suddenly opened and Tom came out wearing his khaki working-smock.

'Gerald . . .' Fell glanced along the street. 'Wasn't that Miss Sherwood?'

'Yes.'

'Pleasant woman. Keeps herself to herself. She goes to the Primitive Methodists, so we don't really know her.'

'Seems she's occupied in looking after her father.'

'And no chance of a match, I expect, till he's off her hands. Pity. She'd likely make some chap a good wife. Not a bad-looking woman. No raving beauty, but not plain either.'

His remarks irritated Hare. He felt there was even a hint of prurience in Fell's discussing in such terms a woman he hardly knew.

'Well, that'll be her business,' he said.

'Oh, aye,' Fell said. 'Hers and some single young chap's. Nothing to do with old married men like you and me.'

Hare was turning to go when Fell went on, 'By the way, Emily spoke on the telephone to your wife.'

'Oh?'

'Seems they've fixed up to go on a jaunt together.'

'A jaunt?'

'Yes. To a horse show, somewhere Wetherby way.'

Hare stood bemused. Well, if it worked and Cynthia made one friend in the town . . . It was no use his yearning for the impossible. He should try to build on what he'd got. And they had been close, in a way, he and Cynthia, for a while. Something, he told himself, *must* happen. They couldn't go on indefinitely as they were.

'Is she interested in horses, then?' Fell was asking.

'She used to ride a little at one time.'

'Well, that's where they're going. Let's hope they have a nice day for it.'

'I decided to take your advice,' Cynthia said, when Hare mentioned it. 'If she wants to be friendly I may as well give it a try.'

'Tom Fell's my oldest friend,' Hare said. 'And his wife's a straightforward warm-hearted woman.'

'Well, we shall see.'

'How will you go?'

'In my car. She doesn't drive.'

He felt himself softening towards her. 'Cynthia,' he said, 'we ought to be able to do better than this.'

'It's a poor lookout if we can't.'

Hare was dozing by the fire, a book in his lap, when the uniformed police sergeant came to the door. He was from the local station and on foot. There had been a bad accident on the A1. The driver of one of the cars was Mrs Hare. No, both she and her passenger were alive but seriously injured. Could Hare tell him who the other woman was?

'It's Tom Fell's wife.'

Hare gave the officer a lift round to Fell's house. Fell had to take the children to his parents before he could leave for the hospital. To Hare's astonishment, he told the girls, still drooping from their disturbed sleep, what had happened. He sat beside Hare on the journey to the hospital, already in a state of shock. 'Oh God, what a terrible thing,' he said over and over. 'Oh God, help us, what a terrible, terrible thing,' until Hare's own nerves were jumping and he forced himself to drive with an exaggerated care that brought Fell to an almost frantic impatience. 'Hurry, Gerald. For God's sake hurry.'

Cynthia was in the operating theatre. Hare was told that she had every chance of recovery and since there was nothing he could do here why didn't he go home and telephone in the morning.

He came upon Fell in a corridor. Fell was leaning against the wall, his face hidden, his shoulders heaving as though he were trying to vomit. Hare touched him. 'Tom . . .' When he turned Hare saw that he was torn by great racking sobs. He got out his words as if they were choking him. 'She's dead, Gerald. Emily's gone. Oh, what am I going to do? Whatever can I do?'

Cynthia came home to her own bed after a fortnight. Hare employed a nurse to look after her while he was out at his business. She had some while ago demanded a room of her own, but now he moved a bed in beside hers so that he would be near her in the night. She became withdrawn, brooding, in a prolonged reflection on her situation. He woke in the middle of one night to find her lying still, eyes wide open, the lamp burning on the far side of her bed.

'Is there anything you want?'

'No.'

'Are you comfortable?'

'Yes.' There was a silence. 'I was just thinking . . .'

'Yes?'

'What a pity it couldn't have been me.'

'What?'

'What a pity she was killed and I was spared.'

'You're talking nonsense.'

'No, I'm not. Your troubles would have been over. You'd have been free.' A silence. 'And so would I.'

Hare took Laura's father's death as an excuse to call on her. She gave him tea.

'I feel quite . . . quite lost without him; without him to care for and think about.'

'Now you can think about yourself for a change.'

'Yes. He'd had a pretty fair innings. Not like poor Mr Fell's wife. That was a terrible shame. How is Mrs Hare?'

'Up and about now. She'll soon be quite her old self.'

'She had a lucky escape.'

'Yes . . . You know that we don't hit it off, Cynthia and I?'

'I didn't, no. I knew she didn't mix much in the town.'

'We virtually live apart.'

'I'm sorry. But God moves in mysterious ways and you've got plenty of time to settle your differences and grow together again.'

'I made a terrible mistake,' Fell said. 'And all I can think now is, if only I'd waited. If only I had.'

'I don't know what you're trying to say to me, but I wish you wouldn't. It really is none of my business.'

'But it is, Laura. I should have waited and come back to you. Do you remember those times before the war, when we used to walk out together?'

'Of course I remember, but – '

'I said nothing then because I was in awe of you.'

'In awe of me?' She laughed. 'Never!'

'Oh, I was. And then the war came and separated us.'

'And then you married and brought a wife home.'

'I still want you, Laura. I want you more than I ever did.'

'You mustn't talk like that. You have a wife.'

'I'm ready to separate from her. I can't go on like this. I'll get a divorce.'

'Do you expect *me* to give her the grounds for that?'

'I'll find a way.'

' "Those whom God hath joined let no man put asunder." I don't believe in divorce.' She turned away and walked across the room. He could see that she was agitated, her face aflame.

'And I've told you, you mustn't come here and talk to me like this.'

'You still cling to all that, do you?' he said. 'The chapel, religion?'

'Of course. Don't you?'

'No. All that mumbo-jumbo was sticking in my throat before the war came, and nothing I saw while I was fighting changed me back. The clergy blessed both sides, you know.'

'You shouldn't blame God for the shortcomings of His followers. Besides, men who might be killed at any time need spiritual comfort, whichever side they fight on.'

'If God exists,' Hare said.

'You don't think he does?'

'They estimate that the Nazis slaughtered six million Jews. What loving father would let that happen to his children?'

'Suffering has always been a mystery,' Laura said. She came and took his cup. 'And now I think you ought to go.'

He got up. One thing, he thought, he would know before he left.

'Laura . . . I want to ask you and I want you to answer me truthfully.'

'You've said enough. Please go now.'

'I want to know . . . If I were free, would you . . . would you favour me?'

She sighed as she moved to rest one hand on the mantelshelf and look into the fire.

'There was a time,' she said finally, 'when I thought a great deal about that. But you're not free, so the question doesn't arise now.'

Cynthia had an older sister who had married and settled in Australia. She wrote to Cynthia in glowing terms of the new life and the glorious weather. Why didn't Cynthia wangle a trip out and recuperate in the sunshine?

'Why don't you go?' Hare said.

'Do you mean it?'

'Of course. Why not?'

'It'd be awfully expensive. And there's the new house.'

'It won't bankrupt me,' Hare said. 'And the house can be ready for you when you get back.'

'Suppose I don't come back?'

'That's up to you. Go by sea. The voyage will do you good.'

'Perhaps it'll give us both a chance to sort ourselves out.'

'Is there nobody else here who'll miss you?' Hare said.

'What do you mean by that?'

But when he shrugged and said no more she did not press him to explain.

Fell was having a hard time coming to terms with Emily's death. His eyes would fill with tears when he spoke of her.

'I still can't get over it, Gerald,' he said. 'Every time I hear the door open I expect her to walk into the room. You're without your wife now, but just imagine to yourself, just close your eyes and imagine that she's gone for good, and you'll have an inkling of what I'm going through.'

'It's no use my pretending that Cynthia and I are as close as you and Emily were,' Hare said. 'You've seen and heard enough to know that.'

'No,' Fell said, 'and to think it was an act of good neighbourliness that brought it about. If only Emily hadn't made that offer. If only she hadn't rung your wife and agreed to go on that trip.' He turned away, choking.

Hare waited till Fell had himself under control.

' "If only", Tom. They're just about the saddest words we have.'

'She was one in a million, Gerald. Nay, in ten million. I'll never replace her. I can't even begin to think of putting anybody else in her place.' ·

'Perhaps not. But you ought to have some kind of help with the girls, you know. There's them to think about as well as you. They've lost a mother, and that they *can* never replace.'

Laura's cottage was a sturdy five-roomed stone building whose fabric her father had had renewed. It stood beside and at an angle to a steep unsurfaced lane, a vehicle's width, down which women from the town took a shortcut to the yarn-spinning mill by the river. On the town side it was almost hidden by an overgrown bank; on the other it looked across the wide valley of river and canal to low wooded hills.

On venturing to visit her again, Hare was glad to find her in the garden. It allowed him to seem merely to be passing and saved him the embarrassment of facing her across her threshold.

'Hullo, there,' he called to her stooping figure.

She straightened up and, momentarily dazzled, shielded her eyes with her hand so that she could see him standing against the sun.

'Hullo.'

'You know, you really have got a marvellous view here.'

'I thought you'd bought the best view in the neighbourhood.'

'You mean with the new house? Something ready-made like this would have saved me the bother.'

'Oh, but your new house will be much more splendid than this.'

'It's a folly,' Hare said. 'A pure grandiose folly.'

'Why did you go to the bother, then?'

'It was my wife's idea. I thought I'd told you.'

'But don't married people come to agreement on such important matters?'

'Some might.'

She was keeping her distance, standing where he had found her. He lifted the gate latch and stepped inside, seeing her head go back an inch.

'You know my wife's gone to visit her sister in Australia?'

'No, I didn't.'

'She thought the change would do her good.'

'After that terrible accident . . .'

'Oh, she's over that now. Quite recovered.'

She wiped a lock of hair off her forehead with the back of her wrist that showed between her gardening-glove and her sleeve. Then she looked down at herself, as if suddenly conscious of the old clothes she was wearing.

'You keep it nice,' Hare said, waving his hand at the garden.

'Father got it established. It was a wilderness when we came, and it would soon be so again.'

He saw that she was uneasy in his presence, but he motioned

to the open door. 'I wonder if I might . . . for a minute.' And when she still did not move or speak. 'There's something I want to talk to you about.'

'I thought we'd had all that out.'

'Please,' Hare said. 'It'll only take a few minutes.'

He followed her, waiting while she removed soil from her flat-heeled shoes on the iron scraper outside the door. When he reached to shut the door behind them, she said, 'Please, I'd rather it were left open.' She didn't offer him a seat.

'I wondered how you were making out on your own,' Hare said. 'How you were managing.' She looked at him, not understanding. 'If there was anything you needed.'

'Are you offering me money?' she said at last.

'I didn't know how your father had left you,' Hare said.

'And what would I be expected to do for it?' She coloured then as Hare looked away. 'I'm sorry. I don't think you deserved that.'

'It would be foolish to be in need when I could help. I shouldn't like the thought of you wanting for anything.'

'It's kind of you. But quite impossible.'

'I don't know why it should be.'

'Oh, but it is. In any case, I might be leaving the district.'

'Leaving?' Hare was startled by the violence with which his heart lurched.

'I'm not destitute, but I must find a way of keeping myself. My mother had relatives in the south. I thought I might get work there.'

'What kind of work?'

'As a housekeeper. Looking after Father all those years has left me fitted for little else.'

'I could probably find you something in the shop.'

'No, please.' A little smile touched her lips.

Panic at the thought of losing her forever brought a thought to Hare.

'Tom Fell needs a housekeeper and a nanny for his girls.'

'Oh?'

'His wife's death hit him badly. He just doesn't seem to be able to reconcile himself to it.' He saw that he had her interest. 'Would you like me to speak to him about it?'

She looked round the room then crossed to the window.

'You don't really want to uproot yourself and go away, do you?'

'I do love this house,' she said eventually. 'I hate the thought of leaving it.'

She stood with her back to him. He went and turned her to face him.

'Stay,' he said. 'Please don't go.'

They had never been so close. Even in the old days he had ventured no more than a steadying hand over a stile. Now he lifted her hot face and bent his towards it. Was he wrong or could she really not hide a hint of softness in her lips before they closed hard against his?

'No.' She twisted free. 'Please go now.'

She went and stood in the open doorway.

'Will you let me speak to Tom?'

'If you like. But I can't stay unless you promise never to come here again.'

A woman passed along the lane, twisting her head to give them a narrow-eyed appraisal as they stepped out of the house.

'It takes only one person to start the tongues wagging,' Laura said.

The telegram arrived when Hare's wife had been away six months. 'Cynthia seriously ill,' it read. 'Letter following but think you should come at once.'

Hare left the business in the hands of his partner and took a flight to Australia. He had nine days in a flying boat in which to wonder just what awaited him. As they flew across the eastern Mediterranean and put down at places he had become familiar with during his first operational posting, he thought, 'When I was here before I didn't even know she existed.'

Cynthia had cancer at an advanced and inoperable stage. There were some new drugs which might arrest it for a time, but she must not be allowed to make that long journey home. Hare was surprised and moved by the courage with which she suffered and fought during the months left to her. She kept active for as long as possible. 'I always used to say life was short, didn't I?' she said. 'Well, now I know just how short, I want to make the most of what's left.'

It was a time of reconciliation, with bitterness gone, and, for

Hare, a strangely ennobling experience. It left him needing time to think and come to terms with himself and his memories. After the funeral he booked a passage home by sea. It was during the long voyage, keeping himself to himself, that he would do his mourning, bury the past and brood on the possibilities of the future.

He came off the train at his local station to find himself on the edge of some farewell party spilling across from the other platform. He recognised one of Fell's daughters. She greeted him shyly.

'Hullo, Elizabeth. What's all this about?'

Before she could reply, Fell himself came round the corner of the station-master's office. 'Elizabeth, the train's due. Don't wander away.' He stopped at the sight of Hare. 'Gerald! How well you look. Fancy you turning up just now!' Fell was dressed in a new suit, a carnation with fern in his buttonhole. 'Come round here a minute.'

He took Hare by the arm and led him along the end of the building. Laura, in a slate-blue two-piece and a hat with its veil turned back, was standing in a group on the other side.

'Laura, look who's here.' She turned her head as the train ran in beside her. 'We got married this morning.' Fell laughed, thumping Hare's back. 'You should have come home earlier and been my best man.'

Laura came to them. It was impossible to read any more in her smile than quiet pleasure. 'Welcome home,' she said.

'Thank you,' Hare said.

'We'd best get on, Tom,' Laura said.

'I hope you'll be very happy,' Hare said.

Now, on the morning after Laura's funeral, Hare was once more in that house through whose rooms he had wandered like a man demented. The weather had changed again.

'It seems,' Fell was saying, 'that we have one calm day for half a dozen blustery ones.' He put coal on the fire then reached for the decanter and topped up Hare's sherry glass and his own.

'It dropped right yesterday, anyway,' Hare said.

'Aye, aye. How does it feel to be back as a visitor in your old home?'

'Strange. Like a memory that won't quite focus.'

'It's been a good home for us. You know,' Fell went on, 'we ·
thought about it afterwards, but that day you ran into me and
Laura on the station, you were, so to speak, coming home
from your own wife's funeral, weren't you?'

'In a manner of speaking, yes.'

'And you never said a word.'

'There was hardly time. And it wasn't a day to burden you
with that kind of news.'

'No. But then, you always kept your feelings to yourself
more than I did.'

'You knew that Cynthia and I hadn't hit it off for some time
before she went to Australia. Though we were, in a way,
reconciled during her illness.'

'Yes. I remember how I was when Emily was killed. Just as
if the world had caved in on me. I didn't know where to put
myself.'

But not this time, seemingly, Hare thought.

'And then,' Fell said, 'you sold out, pulled up stakes and
went off without a goodbye. Whatever made you do that? Too
many uncomfortable memories?'

'Something like that,' Hare said. 'I never really settled down
after the war. Then that spell in Australia, when Cynthia was
dying . . . I felt like a fresh start, where nobody knew me.'

'And you never got married again.'

'No.'

Why shouldn't I tell him? Hare thought. What harm can
there be in it now she's gone? It might even give him some
satisfaction to know the truth. His mind framed the sentences
as Fell looked into the fire, silent, his thoughts elsewhere.

'I went away because I was in love with Laura. I should have
made sure of her before the war, when it looked as if she was
interested and we were both free. But she wouldn't entertain
me while I was tied to Cynthia and she wouldn't hear of me
getting a divorce. When Cynthia died I came home to claim
her, but I was too late. So I left, rather than live in the same
town, seeing her and being constantly reminded what a fool I'd
been.'

That was what he thought of saying, but before he could
start the other man turned from the fire and forestalled him.

'You know,' Fell began, 'we were real friends at one time . . .'

'Still are,' Hare put in, his spoken words followed by the immediate thought: 'But did I ever really *like* him?'

'Yes.' Fell turned his head and gave him an appreciative little smile in which there was a lurking sadness. 'I often think about those years just after the war. They were the golden years, Gerald. For me, at any rate. I know you had your troubles . . . Some men are lucky enough to have a time like that; and luckier still if they recognise it while they're living it. Well, that was my time, and it all fell to pieces when Emily was killed.'

'But surely,' Hare said, 'you've had compensations since.'

'Oh, yes,' Fell conceded. 'Oh, yes; and I'd be churlish not to admit my good fortune in marrying Laura. All the same . . . Well, we have known each other a long time, Gerald, and I can tell you what I wouldn't tell another living soul.'

'But what's wrong with the man?' Hare thought, and felt irritation move in him.

'She was a good wife, Laura,' Fell went on, 'a good woman and a good mother to the girls. And I shall miss her. But somehow, you know, though we were comfortable and never differed in anything that mattered, I sometimes found myself with this feeling of – well, I can only call it disappointment. A feeling that something, somehow, was missing. It was never the same as it was with Emily, you know, and perhaps I was a fool for ever thinking it might be.'

Wind suddenly buffeted the windows and tossed the bare branches of the lime trees in the avenue. Hot coals fell in the fireplace. The two old friends sat silently looking into the flames.

AUTHOR'S NOTE

The Apples of Paradise is a re-working of Thomas Hardy's story *Fellow Townsmen*. I had brooded for some years about an alternative denouement to Hardy's tale, whose irony he either did not see or chose not to use, but which appealed strongly to my own artistic temperament. At first I saw the writing of my own version as no more than an interesting exercise in which I retained some elements of Hardy's plot and planted other clues to its origin in the names of its chief characters. Hardy's are Barnet, Downe and Lucy Savile. Barnet Fair is rhyming slang for hair, or in this case Hare. Downe becomes Fell, and Lucy Savile's initials are retained in those of Laura Sherwood.

While this necessary acknowledgement of its source inevitably emphasises the similarities, and invites disparaging comparison, *The Apples of Paradise*, in its execution, acquired enough independent life to persuade me to offer it for publication.

The Running and the Lame

There were people getting on to the bus before Mrs Brewster was safely off, and the driver was letting them. You got the odd one like that, careless, surly, as though they weren't lucky to *have* a job in times like these. Her walking stick and shopping bag slipped along the stretched arm whose hand clutched the rail while her foot felt for the ground. She wondered with a touch of panic if he would be heedless enough to close the doors on her before she was down and clear. The stick slid free and fell, coming to rest half on, half off the platform, as both her feet touched the ground and she stepped back on to the pavement and regained her balance. Then someone from behind nipped nimbly past her, grasped the stick and put it into her hand, his other hand supporting her elbow.

'You all right, Ma?'

'Thank you,' Mrs Brewster said. 'Thank you very much.'

She peered at him as she waited for her heartbeat to slow, but she had on the wrong glasses for recognising anyone at this range. All she could make out was a youngish man with dark hair, wearing a blue anorak with a broad yellow stripe down the sleeve. God! but she was a mess these days: overweight, short of breath, arthritic in her joints, half blind. Fit for nothing but the knacker's yard, Randolph might have said. It had been one of his 'speaks' that he came out with whatever the company, asking what was vulgar about it when she chided him. She would have to stop coming into town if she couldn't get off a bus without danger. But her local shop had closed six months ago and the neighbours she'd been friendly with had lately moved away. She hated to be dependent on anyone, let alone strangers.

'It's Mrs Brewster, isn't it?' the man asked, and she peered at the pale outline of his face once more.

'Yes. Do I know you?'

'I know you.'

There was no clue in the voice. 'I'm sorry, but I can't place you.'

'That doesn't matter.'

'My eyes aren't what they were.'

She had known so many people in the old days, and many more had known her. Great heavens! she had been mayor of this town and a justice of the peace. All that had happened after Randolph had gone. While he was alive she had been content to back him up; then when he died the Labour Party had offered her his safe seat on the town council. She had taken the gesture as a great compliment, to Randolph as well as herself. How proud he would have been of her, and how distressed to see her now.

'You can manage now, can you?'

'Yes, I'm all right now.'

'I'll be getting on, then.'

'Yes. Thank you for your trouble.'

People weren't all bad, Mrs Brewster thought, as the man walked away. You could think otherwise from all that was reported in the newspapers and on television, and, of course, she had known a lot of cupidity and mischief while she was on the bench; but there was still some politeness and disinterested concern in the world. Helping lame dogs over stiles; helping fat old women off buses.

Mrs Brewster's first errand was to the post office, to draw her pension. On her way across the marketplace she was greeted a couple of times. Sometimes she didn't recognise people who spoke to her, but she always called out a cheery reply. Sometimes, she suspected, she responded when the greeting was not meant for her, but she would rather risk looking foolish than snub someone. 'I saw old Mrs Brewster in town this morning,' she could imagine them saying. 'Blind as a bat, but she still soldiers on.'

As she passed under the bulk of the town hall, the clock in its tower struck a quarter after eleven. Oh! but they'd had some times inside those walls: Mayors' Balls, Chamber of Commerce and Rotary Club dances; brass-band concerts and choirs; the small parties and receptions she herself had held in the Mayor's Parlour during her year of office. She had met Randolph at a dance in there over fifty years ago. He had only recently come into the town to manage his uncle's foundry, which he later inherited. When they had been introduced and had danced together, he took her down to supper in the Winter Gardens. He didn't seem to want to leave her. She felt his gaze on her all evening and he came back to her every time she was for a moment unattended. He told her then that he fancied standing for the council and astounded her by telling her he was a member of the Labour Party. Men who owned or managed businesses stood as Conservatives, or Independents – which was the same thing under another name. Randolph overturned the natural order. Her father, himself a Liberal, said as much later when she wanted to ask Randolph to the house. Randolph had laughed. 'They don't know how to weigh me up. Even my uncle looks at me a bit sideways. "As long as you do your work and don't start wanting to hand the business over to a commune," he says, "I don't see as it makes much difference. Except, o' course, I shan't be able to put you up for t'Conservative Club." '

But the local branch of the party had thought him a catch and let him show what he could do in a ward held by a long-standing and popular Independent whom not even Ernest Bevin or Herbert Morrison could have ousted. He increased the Labour turnout and its vote; then, when John Henry Waterhouse died, they gave him the prize of his safe seat, and she had inherited it in her turn.

Mrs Brewster needed a couple of postage stamps. She hesitated, then paid for first class. She owed a letter to her widowed sister-in-law, who lived in the south, and though what little news she had to write was in no way urgent, she felt that second-class post for personal letters looked mean. The management of the Post Office irritated Mrs Brewster. She could understand their advertising on their own vans, but not their making long and costly TV commercials for overseas telephone calls, or taking quarter-page advertisements in the newspapers for services in which they held a monopoly. It was all a vexation – like the gas bill she went to pay through her bank when she had finished in the post office. She had expected it to be bigger than usual because of the extra heat she had used in the house during that prolonged spell of ferocious weather before Christmas. Bigger it had proved to be, but when she examined it closely and compared it with the equivalent quarter of twelve months before, she found that she had in fact used little more gas, and the extra cost was almost entirely due to increased charges. Oh, she could manage. The provision Randolph had made was, with her pension, sufficient to see her through the time left to her, which couldn't be all *that* long. *She* could manage; but there were others to whom the increasing cost of living was one never-ending fret, and she did not like to imagine what anxiety she might have had to live with were she, say, ten years younger.

From the bank she made her way to the outdoor market where she bought some greens and a small piece of fish. Then to the butcher for a lamb chop and some bacon. Enough to supplement what she kept in her small freezer – which she liked to keep in case she couldn't get out of the house – but not too much to weight her bag till it became a burden.

Now Mrs Brewster could address herself to her shopping-day treat: a bottle of Guinness and a pub lunch, followed, if she felt in the mood, by a glass of port. There was nearly always someone in the Bird in Hand whom she could chat with, though she almost always waited until she was invited before offering her opinion, for she did not want to become one of those boring old people who chipped into every exchange.

The old woman he had helped at the bus stop came into the Bird in Hand as he was sitting up at the bar counter enjoying his first pint of lager. She moved warily in from the door as though expecting traps for her feet, and the landlord called to his black labrador, which had flopped half under one of the tables. 'Now then, Satan,' the old lady said as the dog stood up in her path. He sniffed at then licked the hand which held the walking stick. Transferring the stick, she let the dog nuzzle into the bent fingers. 'Snottynose,' the old woman said. 'Old snottynose.' 'He knows you, all right,' the landlord said. He had already uncapped a small bottle of Guinness and was carefully pouring it as, casually wiping her hand on the rough tweed of her coat, she approached the counter. 'Oh, he knows *me*,' she said. Mrs Brewster. After all these years. She'd felt she ought to know *him*. And so she should.

'Will you be partaking of lunch?' the landlord asked as he picked out the money for the drink from the loose change she had spread on the counter and rang open the till.

'Steak sandwich and chips,' Mrs Brewster said. 'Ask Maisie to brown the onions. No hurry. Whenever she's ready. I'm not to ten minutes.'

The landlord went and called the order into the back and Mrs Brewster took her glass and turned to choose a seat, nodding 'Good morning' as she faced the man at the bar. There was no one else in the room.

'Morning.'

She peered at him, her eyes narrowing. 'Are you the young man who rescued my walking stick?'

'Yes.'

'You've still got the advantage of me.'

'You were well known at one time.'

'At one time, yes. Those days are over now, though.'

'Nobody gets any younger, Mrs Brewster,' the landlord put in as he came back and started to pull another half-pint into his own glass.

'You two have still a bit further to go than me,' Mrs Brewster said.

'That's something nobody can be sure of.'

'No, you're quite right,' Mrs Brewster conceded. 'And it wouldn't do for us to know such things.' She stood for a moment, turned in on her thoughts, before asking the man at the bar, 'Do you live here?'

'I used to.'

He saw that she was still no wiser. It would nag her now, but he thought she wouldn't like to pester him with more direct questions.

She turned away and moved to sit down as he looked past her and through the window to where Eric was getting out of the rusting L-registered Marina he had just driven into the yard. Eric ran his hand round the waistband of his trousers, tucking in his shirt, then hoicking the trousers up as he walked out of sight round the corner of the building. The man at the bar had emptied his glass and ordered a refill and was holding money when Eric stuck his head and one shoulder round the door.

'Now then.'

'How do, Eric. What'll you have?'

'Oh, the same as you.'

Eric was holding his hands as though he half expected to be asked to shake; then he employed them to go again through the motion of tucking down his shirt and pulling up his trousers which, like his jacket, were stained with engine oil.

'Been losing weight, or do you buy your suits secondhand?'

Eric rested one hand on his belly. 'Got rid of a bit o' beer gut.'

'Not much chance of a beer gut where I've been.'

Eric shot a quick glance at the landlord, who was at the till, as the other man took a deep swig of his fresh pint.

'You don't look too bad on it, anyway.'

'Like the tan, do you?'

Eric drank. 'What's on your mind, then?'

'Let's go where we can talk.' He got off the stool and led the way to a table down the room.

'It won't be as quiet as this for long,' Eric said, following.

'Perhaps it won't take long.'

Eric took out a green tobacco tin. He slipped a paper from its packet, laid tobacco along it and began to roll a smoke. The other man watched him fumble for a couple of seconds then reached across. 'Give it here.' His deft fingers evened the lie of the tobacco, then closed the paper into a neat cylinder. He held it out to Eric with the gummed edge free. 'Lick.'

Eric said 'Thanks' and pushed the box across the table. The other man pushed it back.

'Broke that habit long since.'

Eric lit up, inhaled, took a drink of lager, all with quick, restless movements. The other man sat hunched at the table, both hands lightly touching the cold moist outside of his glass.

'What made you come back here?' Eric asked. 'Been me, this is the last place I'd've come to.'

'Been you, Eric, you wouldn't have been where I've been.'

'Been me, there'd've been no need for any of it.'

'Still kidding yourself about that, are you? Still think if she'd married you first she wouldn't have taken somebody else on?'

'She's been all right with me all this time.'

'But she'd had the fright of her life, lad.' His gaze took in Eric's jacket. 'That's a good whistle and flute. Or it was at one time. Still like to dress nice, I see.'

'Never took in the jeans bit,' Eric said. 'I've spent enough time in overalls. I like to make an effort when I go out.'

'Does *she* still like her nights out?'

'Well . . .' Eric looked at his hands. 'You can't do all you might like when you've got young 'uns.'

'Oh, yes, the young 'uns. Two, aren't there?'

'That's right. Two lads.'

'Two lads. Happy families.'

'You had your chance.'

'What chance was that?'

'If you couldn't make her happy . . .'

'You self-satisfied bastard. You think you'd've done any better? She'd have made mincemeat of you, the woman she was then.'

'Happen so. Happen not.'

'You got the leavings, mate. What was left after me and that other bastard.'

'You're still not sorry, I see.'

'I'd've swung for the bastard. Her an' all.'

'There were plenty thought you should have.'

'Well, I didn't. And now I'm out.'

'So what's it all been for? What are you after, coming back here?'

'That's what I thought I'd find out.'

'It's all done with, a long time ago.'

'You'd know how long it's been if you'd lived every day of it like I have.'

'Me heart bleeds.'

'I want to see her, Eric.'

Eric shook his head. 'No. You can't.'

'Has she said so?'

'She doesn't want to see you.'

'Has she *said* so?' he asked again. 'Does she know I'm out?'

'We don't talk about you.'

'She must have known my time was about up.'

'We've never talked about it.'

'So you didn't tell her I'd been in touch with you?'

'No.'

'What are you scared of?'

'Raking up what's dead and buried.'

'Hasn't she got a mind of her own? Since when did you do her thinking for her?'

'*I* look after her now.'

'You're taking a lot on yourself.'

'If you think she's still pinin' for you, you're mistaken.'

'I'd like her to speak for herself, Eric.'

'After what you did? You must be barmy to think she'd give you the time o' day.'

'What's to stop me waiting on the street for her?'

'I can always set the police on to you. They'd make you leave us alone.'

'You'd enjoy that, wouldn't you? But she'd have to know then. Why don't you just do it the easy way and give her a message: tell her I'd like to see her.'

'What will you do when she says no?'

'I'll cross that bridge when I come to it.'

'Christ!' Eric said, 'but you do fancy yourself, don't you? All this has learned you nowt, has it?'

'I've done my time, Eric. I've paid for what I did.'

'Paid? They've let you out, but who says you've paid? Do you think *she* thinks you've paid?'

'That's up to her to say. You can't talk for her on that.' He paused while he drank, long and deep. 'You're taking too much on yourself, Eric. Tell her I want to see her.'

'You haven't even asked how she is. D'you think time's stood still for everybody while you've been inside?'

'Have her looks started to go, then? Do you make enough to give her what she wants, or has she been working her fingers to the bone for you?'

'We do all right.'

'I should doubt it, from the look of that clapped-out wreck you drove up in.'

'It happened to be the one in the yard with the keys in it. Tomorrow it could just as easy be a Merc.'

'Go on, Eric, impress me. You buy cars at auction, patch 'em up and flog 'em for a few quid more to suckers who don't know any better.'

'And what bright golden future have you come out of nick to? I don't know whether you've heard, but we're in a recession. There's over three million unemployed. What have you got to offer her, even if she wanted it?'

'Who says I want to offer her anything? Who says I want *her*?'

'What the hell do you want, then?'

'I want to see her. How is she?'

Eric took a deep breath. 'She's dying.'

'You what?'

'It's cancer.'

'Go on.'

'It started a couple of years ago, in one breast. They hoped they'd caught it in time.'

'I don't believe you.'

'Believe what you like. I never knew it was like that. Sometimes she's nearly like normal, except she's thinner and easy tired. Other times she has to stop in bed. Soon she'll be in bed for good – for what time there is left.'

'How long do they give her?'

'She won't see another Christmas.'

'Steak sandwich and chips, Mrs Brewster.' The landlady put the plate on the table with a knife and a fork wrapped in a paper napkin. 'I hope I haven't kept you waiting.'

'No, no. No hurry. I'm just nicely ready for it now. You're quiet today.'

'There'll be a few more in later. But it's the schools' half-term. We're always a bit quieter then.'

'Maisie . . .' Mrs Brewster leaned in over the table as the woman turned to go. 'Do you know that chap over there, the one looking this way?'

'Can't say I know either of them. I noticed them as I came through from the kitchen. They're not falling out, are they?'

'They're not bothering anybody else, if they are. No, he seemed to know me and I've this feeling I ought to know him.'

'Didn't you ask him who he was?'

'I gave him plenty of chance to tell me, but he didn't let on. It's these blessed eyes of mine lately; they miss so much they wouldn't have missed at one time. He said he used to live here.'

'Well, of course, we haven't been here long.'

'No, well . . .'

'Have you got everything you want? Would you like some mustard, or vinegar?'

'No, just salt and pepper. Thank you.'

He tapped his empty glass with a fingernail and waited for Eric to take the hint.

'D'you want another?'

'How much is brandy these days?'

'About the same as this.'

'Wouldn't want you to be out of pocket. I'll have a brandy.'

'Any particular brand?'

'I'm not fussy.'

He was feeling light in the head, as though dizziness might strike him if he stood up. Well, he was out of practice. But two pints of lager shouldn't have got to him like that.

Cancer. And they'd already had the knife into her.

Across the room Mrs Brewster was eating her food and wiping juice from her chin with her paper serviette. She twisted her head and looked at him. The sunlight through the window behind her turned her glasses into two impenetrable discs of reflected light, but he thought her mouth curved in a little smile.

She had not smiled that day he had faced her in the magistrates' court in the town hall, when they sent him up to the crown court on a charge too grave for them to try. Her mouth had worked then as the police gave the evidence and she heard just what he'd done. He'd thought she was having all on not to be sick. There was more than one in the room that day who would cheerfully have marched him out to the marketplace and topped him there and then. And now she couldn't place him.

Eric had got the drinks and paid for them. He left them on the bar and went through the door he had entered by. As the landlord stepped into the back room, the other man suddenly got up and walked to the bar. He took the brandy and threw it back in one; then, without looking at Mrs Brewster, he went out.

There were doors in the passage marked LADIES and GENTS. He walked past them and into the street.

Mrs Brewster tried to poke a scrap of lettuce from under her top denture with her tongue. She would have to go and rinse it. She drank the last quarter-inch of her Guinness and considered whether or not to buy a glass of port. It was dull in the Bird in Hand today. Boring. She would have been better occupied in eating a snack at home while watching *Pebble Mill at One* on television.

One of the men came back, the one who had come in last. He went to the bar counter and only looked behind him at the table where he had been sitting when he saw the empty brandy glass.

'He went out,' Mrs Brewster said.

'Oh.'

This man remained standing at the bar. He bit at one of his fingernails before drinking.

'He must have gone,' Mrs Brewster said.

'Yes . . . Aye . . .'

'Should I know him?' Mrs Brewster asked; but the man was now in a study and seemed not to have heard her. Then he suddenly turned his head.

'Did you say something?'

'I said I thought I ought to know him.'

'Oh, he's nobody you'd be interested in, love,' Eric said.

The Middle of the Journey

Dear Monica,

So you heard. I didn't want to alarm you or upset you without real cause so I decided I'd wait until I had something positive to tell you. I've always known how fond you are of Raymond, though it was believing your friendship for me came first that led me to unburden myself to you all those years ago and only afterwards did I realise that I'd not behaved with the last ounce of tact in choosing you as my confessor. But then, confession itself can often be construed as a selfish act, can't it, and what in the end are friends for was what you said to me yourself at the time. So here I go again, because at the moment you can only know what everyone else knows, not what else came out of it.

We were driving up the A1 to Yorkshire and I was telling Raymond that I couldn't remember travelling so far north in England since I'd visited my Aunt Lally, in Harrogate, as a child. But, of course, I could. 'I've passed through on the train to Scotland, but that hardly counts.'

Raymond said the trains are so frequent and fast nowadays he'd been tempted to suggest we should travel that way.

'You'd have had to pay carriage on the wine,' I reminded him.

'True. And they're just that bit off the beaten track, which would have put them to the trouble of meeting us.'

The man we were going to stay with has a house in the country, with a large cellar. He had put it to Raymond that with the number of free-house pubs and well-to-do families in the area an agency for quality wines could be run from his home, and Raymond, looking for a foothold in that region, had agreed to give it a try, though he had wondered aloud to me whether our host's immediate interest extended any further than the possibility of making enough profit to cover his own wine bill.

'Anyway, with the car,' I pointed out, 'we can leave when we like, should anything go wrong.'

'Wrong?'

'If we're bored by them, or they're bored by us; or the food's awful, or the beds are damp.'

'You're becoming a regular fusspot, Nora.'

'No, I'm not. But I do know the minimum I need to keep me comfortable and contented, and I can't throw myself into these adventures with the blithe abandon I used to.'

'Adventures! A weekend in the country with a potential customer? Blithe abandon? Whenever did blithe abandon win over your natural caution?'

'You'd be surprised,' I wanted to say, 'astounded if I confessed to you now.' I hadn't thought about it for years. Well, not to let it preoccupy me for more than two or three consecutive minutes. It was only this journey to that part of the country which had brought it back. Not that we were going to the same part exactly, either: it was a good thirty miles away. I'd checked it on the map before telling myself that it wouldn't have mattered if we'd been bound for the same hotel: no one would have been likely to remember after all that time.

But I remembered: I remembered more than I'd known I could, giving myself the luxury of sitting down and *letting* myself remember; safe now at this distance of years.

Raymond was telling me what the country was like: 'Farming land; great sweeps of it. Rich. Well wooded in parts. It's not like the Dales, you know. People who don't know Yorkshire think everything outside the cities is barren moors and the Dales.'

Oh, yes, the Dales. The weather had been atrocious, but we had hardly cared. We had walked in wind and rain and exclaimed as occasional sunshine lit vistas we had resigned ourselves to not seeing. Four bracing days, three blissful nights. (Did I tell you all this? Enough of it, anyway.) It seemed to *me* like abandon, though I'd banished guilt by an act of will. Raymond was on a buying trip in France. Douglas and I were a long way from home, and he had chosen well: a place he'd called on a couple of years before and remembered. I'd tried teasing him, asking him if he'd brought someone else here, before.

'It struck me as a good place for a honeymoon.'

A honeymoon. Ah . . .

'Not for young people who need nightlife, theatres, bright lights,' he said, 'but for a mature couple who are content with each other.'

Yes, a honeymoon . . .

Douglas, as you know, had married and divorced young. 'It didn't take,' he said. 'Thank goodness we were both sensible enough to let go before any lasting damage was done.' He'd been bitten once and now trod warily. I was no threat to him. We didn't speak of the future – not then. The present was everything and life too short to deny ourselves the pleasure we gave each other. Many a lasting marriage has been under-pinned by a little outside excitement, I'd told myself. Douglas had seemed to understand; to want and expect no more than that.

Until he spoke of honeymoons, and then, the imagination being what it is, my thoughts began to reconstruct our affair as a trial run for a venture on which I knew we both would have happily embarked were there nothing in the way.

Only Raymond, of course. No children, and likely to be none. Not much passion, either, if the truth be told – and now was the time to tell it – but a gentle, companionable union which I'd thought contained all I should ever need for the rest of my life.

'Do whatever you think is best for you,' you said to me. 'Do it and abide by it.' And only much later did it occur to me how hard it might have been for you not to say straight out, 'Go with Douglas, if you want him so much.' For that would have freed Raymond so that you and he might . . . Well, not then, but later, in the fullness of time. (Am I imagining all that? Forgive me if I am. But you may never have allowed yourself to frame the thought so clearly.)

Raymond came back from France with tales of the wife of the vineyard owner he had bought from. 'She seemed to me to be a woman who had all a woman could reasonably hope for: good looks, three healthy children, a well-to-do and respected husband who obviously loves her. And what is she? A cold, arrogant shrew. If he didn't love her so much and hadn't his work, which is his passion, I suspect he would have to acknowledge that she does her level best to make his life a misery. All I could think of was how very, very lucky I am to have you and how very, very easy it must be to make a mistake that could ruin one's life.'

He wanted me that night and something in me responded so that I opened myself freely and worked to quicken our feeling. He was grateful. 'Well, old girl,' he said afterwards, 'I rather think you must have been missing *me*.'

Douglas said I wanted both of them. 'I want you,' I told him, 'but I can't hurt him.'

'You're going to have to choose.'

'Oh, why didn't you say all this at the beginning?'

'I didn't know at the beginning. But now you must choose.'

'Not yet, Douglas,' I said. 'Please, not just yet.'

And then one day, as you know, I went to where he should have been and he wasn't there. I waited for his message – I had to leave it to him. None came. It was over.

Perhaps you can see that for Raymond to tease me about my 'natural caution' was to tempt me, with the ache long gone, to diminish my sacrifice: to let in the small voice which insinuated that caution had indeed been my prime motive, that saving virtue of common sense which had told me, even in deepest thrall, which side my bread was buttered on.

Because I did get my reward, you know. I got what I'd always wanted as a girl: marriage to a gentle and totally reliable man and a civilised life in which I could read the books I wanted to read, see the films and the plays, take my seat at the opera, travel, tend my garden, entertain his friends, mine, ours, in a home where money was never a pressing problem.

So why was I feeling so strongly at this late stage (because of where we were going, because of the memories the journey had resurrected, because of his light-hearted jibe about my 'caution'?) the urge to tell him how it had all been bought and paid for?

I offered to drive for a spell, but I knew he didn't want me to.

He didn't mind long journeys so long as he was at the wheel, but he was a poor passenger and soon began that tuneless humming that might have sounded to others like contentment, but which I knew as a sure sign he was ill at ease.

I, on the other hand, perfectly relaxed physically, felt sleep reach for me. As my head rolled and jerked, Raymond said why didn't I let the seat down and take a nap.

'Sure you don't mind?'

'Not a bit.'

'I always feel such a cheat, napping while someone else is driving.'

'And I always say I don't mind.'

'Well, if you won't let me drive.'

'Take your nap. I'll put the radio on.'

'We can stop for coffee whenever you wish.'

I knew in my sleep that the car had stopped, which was what woke me. I took in slowly as I stretched and yawned that we were not on a hotel or snack-bar forecourt, but by the roadside, as a massive container lorry whooshed by with a warning blare of horn, shuddering even the sturdy Volvo where it stood, and drowning for the moment the inane voices on a local radio phone-in programme.

I turned my head, starting to ask 'What . . .?' and sitting bolt upright as I saw him.

He couldn't speak. I wasn't even sure he could hear me. The spasm seemed to have left him; his hands still clung to the wheel and his eyes stared straight ahead, looking at God only knew what, out of a face bloated with a colour the like of which I'd never seen before and hope and pray I shall never see again.

There was no moving him to get to the wheel myself. I wondered how much warning he'd had and as I switched off the radio and loosened his tie and spoke to him again, I knew that I had no idea at all how to take the first steps in such an emergency; I mean what was dangerous, what might make the difference between life and death.

I made out what looked like a pub sign some way in front and opened the door. 'Raymond, I'm going to get help.' As I got out I thought to reach back, turn off the ignition and switch on the hazard warning lights. Then I ran, stumbling at first along the rough grass shoulder before I risked taking to the edge of the road itself.

The doctor was explaining to me: 'A lot of things – even familiar things – have become jumbled – scrambled, you could call it – in his mind. He couldn't get his own name right this morning.'

'Good lord!'

'He's not going *out* of his mind,' he went on quickly. 'You mustn't worry about that. It's quite a common effect of a seizure and in a day or two it should sort it self out.'

'He *is* going to be all right, isn't he?'

'Oh, yes; with treatment and rest he should be back to normal quite soon. I say normal, though you'll both have to regard what's happened as a warning and see that he adjusts his way of life accordingly.'

It was the first time I'd spoken with this man – the specialist. At first it had been the staff in Casualty, too brisk and preoccupied to tell me anything.

'You don't live hereabouts?'

'No, our home's in Surrey. We were on our way to visit some business connections of my husband's, in Yorkshire.'

'But you've found a place to stay?'

'I'm in a motel, just outside town. They have my phone number on the ward.'

I wanted to ask him more, but I guessed he'd told me all he could – or wanted to – for the present. His telephone pinged as though it was about to ring. He moved some papers on his desk. He was a busy man. I got up and left him.

Devilishly expensive it was, too, the place I'd booked myself into that first fraught day, taking the easiest course and choosing from the hotel guide that Raymond carried in the car. Comfortable, of course, with a private bathroom, colour television and a refrigerator stocked with enough drink to keep anyone paralytic for a week. And a drink was what I felt I needed, limp as I was with relief that Raymond was going to be all right, and suspended now in a kind of limbo, not knowing how long we must stay in this strange place halfway to our destination.

I chose whisky. I mustn't get drunk. A couple in my present state would make me tipsy. Oh God! Oh, thank God, thank God he was going to be all right (and he is, Monica, he is; I assure you). Just how much I needed him had been made plain to me on that roadside as the ambulancemen took him from the car and I stood, transfixed by pure terror at the possibility of losing him.

It was the weekend now. Raymond's office was closed and I couldn't remember the home telephone number of his partner. I must also ring the Ascoughs, who would be wondering what on earth had happened to us.

'I need some phone numbers, Raymond,' I'd said to him at the hospital.

His address book would be in his briefcase, which was now with our luggage, in my hotel room. The case was one of those rigid-framed leather ones with numbered tumbler locks.

But all he'd done was smile, in a distant, dreamy fashion, as though he were far away, in a private place I couldn't reach. I'd hesitated to press him. And if, as the specialist had said, he couldn't unscramble his own name, how could his confused mind be expected to yield the six figures which would open the case?

I put the case on the low table and looked at it. With so many arbitrary combinations of figures assigned one in this computer age, he'd surely for himself have chosen a sequence he could readily recall. I tried his birthday. No. His office telephone number was seven figures. I tried the first six, then the last. I did the same with our home number, then I had a drink of whisky and looked out of the window. It was a lovely day. The land was green. I'd promised myself some country walks while Raymond did his business. What could the Ascoughs be thinking?

It was lunchtime, but I didn't feel like going to the restaurant. Ringing room service, I ordered soup and a salad sandwich. Coffee or tea I could make here in the room.

When I'd filled the kettle and plugged it in, then poured the rest of the whisky from the miniature and added another cube of ice, my gaze fell on the television set. I switched on and sat down opposite it. From where I sat I could see my reflection in the glass over the dressing-table unit. I wondered again at the face that had led a man to lead me astray and asked myself what Douglas would have made of it now. Well, I'd experienced that. I'd known it, was the better for it, and no harm done. For now I'd something to measure it against.

There was a magazine programme on television. They were talking about a new picture biography of the Princess of Wales and showing film of her wedding day. It was when my food had arrived and I was thanking the waiter and looking for my handbag while wondering if I'd remembered aright that service was included, that a thought slipped into my mind.

I let the food stand and the kettle come to the boil as I rolled the tumblers of Raymond's case and clicked the locks open.

Then I was crying and choking as I tried to swallow what was left of the whisky. That he should have chosen that combination. That *that* should be the sequence he lined up every day when he opened the case. The date of *our* wedding.

'Oh God, but that's touching!'

I'd spoken out loud. Because he'd reached me. Not knowing, he'd reached me as surely as if he'd placed a gentle fingertip on my cheek.

His partner wanted to drive up straight away. I put him off. 'Don't trouble, Eldon. There's nothing you could do. Tomorrow or the day after they may let me take him home. The specialist seemed quite optimistic.' I said nothing about the scrambling of Raymond's mind. Eldon is a fussy and pedantic man and a careless word about that could lead him to wonder if Raymond would be capable of pulling his weight again.

The Ascoughs' phone was answered by a girl with a thick foreign accent.

'Is nobody here,' she said. 'All out.'

I spoke slowly and clearly. 'Will you give them a message, please. This is Mrs Raymond Hawkridge. They were expecting us. My husband was taken ill on the journey and now we must cancel our visit. I'll ring them later, when I have more news. Will you make sure they get that message?'

'Will do,' the girl said, and hung up.

My soup had gone cold but I didn't mind. Soup of the day, which I'd not troubled to identify, had turned out to be tomato, which always gives me indigestion. Munching my sandwich, I boiled the kettle again and made tea. Before very long it would be time to take the car and visit Raymond once more.

I must ask him, try to get him to tell me, if there was anything I should do. Before that, was there anything in his briefcase I might need? I hadn't closed it. Its lid stood open, held by brass hinges. A handsome case, which I'd given him myself, with a mock-suede lining and leather loops holding pens. Two folders lay neatly in the base; other papers were tucked into two pockets in the lid.

I told myself that it was not my way to pry; but until I looked I could have no idea what might be important and what not. Ludicrously, as it seemed then, the old saw came to mind that those who eavesdrop seldom hear good of themselves. And then a moment later colour was flooding my throat and face. They burned as though I'd been caught shamelessly delving.

I was holding an envelope drawn from deep in one of the pockets – an envelope already slit open, though addressed to myself. I found that I could still hear his carefully modulated voice (an old-fashioned actor's voice, I used to tease) as I read what was inside (and which you, Monica, since I've come so far, may as well hear too):

'My dear Nora, I knew you would know it was finished when I didn't come to our usual place, and I knew that after all we'd said you would make no attempt to contact me. I thought it best that way, but now I feel I must say a final word.

'I am oddly bitter that you were ready to throw away what we found together. You speak of duty and moral choices as if they were absolutes handed down from on high, when you don't believe that any more than I do. I can't for the life in me see what you owe someone who has left such a void in *your* life, you have had to snatch at happiness elsewhere. Yours isn't a nature that craves the excitement of an adventure, yet you haven't the courage to grasp what is being offered to you. I hope you won't spend the rest of your life regretting it.

'For myself, I shall be a long time forgetting. As a start, I'm going abroad. I had the offer of this job before. Had things gone differently I should have taken you with me. Now I shall go alone. Who was it said there was nothing like a sea-change for putting an unhappy relationship in perspective? We shall see.

'The "decent" thing now would be for me to thank you for the great joy you gave me. I would, but it's been too dearly bought. I always said your Raymond didn't deserve you. Now I think perhaps he does. Goodbye. D.'

I got up then and went to the window and took several deep breaths, until my heart stopped racing.

Of course, I wondered how he'd come to intercept it and why he chose then to keep it from me. Not that there was anything in it that I hadn't already known and come to terms with. But why, when he'd decided not to face me with it, did he not destroy it? Why keep it and carry it with him? To remind himself of the perfidy of women? That what you trusted most was least to be trusted? Or did he find in that ever-present knowledge that I'd been tempted yet turned back to him his greatest solace?

Dear Monica, I'm putting all this down because I have to try to get it clear in my mind, and that's best done as if I were talking to someone; someone who knew. But I doubt if I shall post this letter. Not this one, but another, a simpler one, appreciating your anxiety and putting your fears at rest. It's really too late in the day for me to let myself wonder whether there was a moment when temptation led you to try to turn things to your advantage.

But how bitter for you, as well as us, if there was. Because for myself, you see now, I have to come to terms with the realisation that Raymond has been living all these years not with the woman I let him know, but with one he knew as well as she knew herself. And I'm going to have quite enough to think about learning to live with that.

Rue

He lived alone in the house after his wife died. They had not got on for years and he was vaguely surprised when he found that she had made no will, so that everything came to him: what was left of her father's money, his collection of snuff-boxes, all she had owned. He had often wondered what it would be like to leave her; but the loneliness in the house after she died was appalling. The silence was the worst; that and opening the door to a room and knowing she would not be there. Her absence was like the ache in an amputated limb.

He was the managing director of a printing firm, was paid a director's fee on top of a substantial salary and was given a new car every two years. Fifty-three years old now, he would retire at sixty with a pension and a block of shares in the company.

Always reserved, he had many acquaintances but no close friends. The people who visited the house had come to see his wife. They stopped coming when she died and he thought they must have been relieved when he did not take up the invitations to dinner parties and the like which they sent him in the early days of his widowerhood.

A woman had come in two half-days in the week to help with the cleaning. He gave her his wife's key so that she could let herself in, but after a short time she left a note to say she would not be coming any more. He went to see her, wondering if he had offended her in some way and ready to offer her more money. She did not express herself clearly, but he gathered that she did not like the empty house either, preferring company while she worked.

At night he lay awake in his bed straining his ears for every small sound as the house cooled.

He thought about moving. He could sell the house at a handsome profit, buy a flat and invest the rest of the money. But he dreaded finding himself at the mercy of neighbours, who might have children, might quarrel, might play pop music into the night. He had always prized the quiet of the house, but not this silence. It was as though what the house lacked now was the sound of his wife's breathing.

There had been one child, a boy, who died in a swimming accident in his early teens. His wife had blamed him for that, said he could have saved the lad. In time he came to believe it himself. He found that he could no longer touch her. From being a tired routine, their intimate life died altogether. He gave himself occasional relief and tried not to let the subject preoccupy him.

Now he thought about the new relationships his freedom made possible and began to take stock of himself. He had felt middle-aged for years, but though he was a little overweight (he had always inclined to tubbiness), he still had his teeth, most of his hair, and managed without glasses except for reading. He took note of the age of politicians and others who came into the news, looked at them on television and compared his appearance with theirs.

He took up jogging. He bought a tracksuit and the right kind of shoes and at first drove out of the neighbourhood and began with short runs which would not put too much sudden strain on his heart. As the nights drew in, he also started trotting round the local streets, last thing. This served the double purpose of giving him exercise and tiring him for bed.

One night, after dark, he was stopped and questioned by two policemen, in a car. They asked him his name and address and what he did for a living. There was a man going about murdering women on the streets. He had been doing it for five years. Jordan realised when they had let him go what a good disguise the role of a jogger could be. It was natural for a jogger to be seen running; he could carry his weapons on a belt under his tracksuit and remove any blood from the suit by putting it straight into the washer.

Still the nights troubled him. It was then that he felt his

loneliness most. He tried comparing his loneliness with that of
a man who was impelled to murder strange women. It did not
help him much.

He tried taking a nip of Scotch before going to bed and
gradually increased his consumption until one night,. when he
had drunk a third of a bottle, he realised he was talking to
himself. His mind, calm and concentrated at work, slipped late
at night into a turmoil. When he had had a lot to drink he felt
that there was something that made sense of everything lying
just beyond the grasp of his thoughts. That was what whisky
did to him, and drinking alone.

He had never frequented public houses but one evening,
having noted the warmly lighted windows of the local at the
end of the street, he forewent his run and walked along there
instead. About to order Scotch, he changed his mind and asked
for a pint of bitter. It was cool and palatable, making a good
mouthful. He stayed an hour, standing at one end of the bar
counter, and drank three pints. He felt the tension gradually
drain out of him. His thoughts drifted. He vaguely recognised
several people he had seen in the neighbourhood. A couple of
them nodded to him, but none of them struck up a conversation. The barmaid, whom he had never seen before, wished
him goodnight as he left. Her hair was the colour of partly
burned corn-stubble. Her top teeth protruded slightly and her
tongue occasionally flicked saliva from the corners of her lips,
which remained apart in respose. Her sudden smile as she
reached for his glass and dipped it into the washing-up
machine behind the bar remained with him as he strolled home
and let himself into the empty house.

He thought about her as, too sleepy to read more than half a
page, he switched off his bedside light; and again when his
radio-alarm woke him out of a deep, unbroken sleep. His
bladder was full and as he padded briskly along the landing to
the bathroom he wondered how old she was and tried to
remember whether she had worn a wedding ring.

He had a ticket for the opera that evening. It was his greatest
interest outside his work. There had been a time when he
thought his wife enjoyed it too. But when he played gramo-

phone records from his considerable collection or tuned in to a radio broadcast, she found excuses to do other things, and he began to realise that she had little ear for music and that only the stage spectacle made it tolerable for her. Latterly, she had sneered at what she called opera's 'unreality' and people standing about 'bawling their heads off'. He had found solace in shutting himself in another room and escaping through music into the world each score conjured up. Yet since her death he could not concentrate for more than a few minutes. Without her unsympathetic presence in the house, his thoughts wandered and even those favourite passages which could start to sing in his mind at any moment of the day slid by only half noticed.

Tonight he saw a performance of Verdi's *Don Carlos* in a new production not yet run in, with small troubles that lengthened the intervals and kept the audience late. He had thought of calling at his local for a last drink, but by the time he had driven up out of the city the pub was closed.

Lights still burned inside where the staff would be washing glasses and clearing up. He wondered if the woman lived on the premises and, if not, how she got home and how far she had to go. His wife would have called her common, a millgirl, and pointed with distaste to the unnatural colour and spoiled texture of her hair. Yet he could not forget the direct genuineness of that smile, and 'genuine' was the one word he found himself applying to her.

When he went into the pub the next evening, there was a woman serving whom he took to be the publican's wife. He did not like to ask how often the other woman was on duty and when she would be here again. They might have several casual staff for all he knew, and he had no name with which to identify the woman with the corn-stubble hair and that appealing open smile. Nor was she there on either of the two crowded weekend nights. He was being silly, behaving like an adolescent. She was no different from any number of the women employed at the works. He must have sunk low in personal resource if he could be so affected by a single friendly smile from a complete stranger. If the pub had been any farther away, he would not have returned. But it was so convenient. He had taken to the beer and he liked the atmosphere. But not at weekends. Then there were too many people, too much noise and tobacco smoke. He was constantly jostled at the bar as he stood aside to let people get served.

He had other things to think about. He must work out a way of living instead of drifting from day to day. The house was becoming neglected. Every Saturday morning he dusted and vacuumed, but knew that it needed more than that. He had pinned a typewritten postcard advertising his need of a cleaner to the works' noticeboard, hoping that one of the women would know someone who wanted the work, but there was no response. Now he redrafted it as a small ad for the evening paper: 'Widower (businessman) requires cleaner, two sessions a week (no heavy work). Old Church Road area. References. Telephone outside business hours.'

She rang on a payphone when the ad had appeared three times. 'Are you the man that's wanting a cleaner?'

'Yes, I am.'

'Can I ask you what two sessions a week means?'

'Two mornings or two afternoons, whichever is more convenient.'

'No evenings?'

'Well, no.'

'That's all right, then. I've got an evening job.'

'You could probably combine the two nicely.'

'Yes . . .' There was a silence, as if she were thinking, or trying to assess him from his voice.

'Are you interested?'

'It is a genuine advertisement, isn't it?'

'What do you mean?'

'There's some funny folk about these days. You've got to be careful.'

'My wife died six months ago,' Jordan said. 'Things have been getting out of hand.'

'Hmm. I suppose I'd better come over.'

'When can you come?'

'Would tonight be all right? I'm not working tonight.'

'That's all right. Where are you speaking from?'

She told him a district of the city that was about twenty minutes away by bus and he gave her the number of the house.

'Shall I give you directions?'

'Is it anywhere near the Beehive?'

'It's just round the corner. Five minutes away.'

'I'll find it, then.'

'I'll expect you.'

'By the way, what's your name?'

'Jordan.'

'I'll be seeing you, then.'

He supposed it would mean nothing to this woman, but he had very occasionally to remind people in whom his name touched a distant chord of memory that he shared it with the hero of a Hemingway novel. 'Except that you don't look like Gary Cooper,' a local academic – a lecturer in American literature at the university – had once remarked. 'And I've certainly never had the pleasure of sharing a sleeping bag with Ingrid Bergman,' Jordan had added.

That had been at a gathering in the neighbourhood he'd been taken to by his wife. He supposed they still went on, those Sunday morning or early evening sherry parties, but he was never asked to them now. You could live very privately in these tree-lined roads of stone houses in what had once been a village with a couple of miles of open land between it and the city. That had suited him: he was a private man. But that had been before the loneliness which assailed him after his wife died. Perhaps, he thought, now, if he could get some help in the house he would give a party himself, renew some acquaintanceships, meet some new people. He did not want to think about living much longer as he was doing now.

He had already eaten a light supper and now he washed his hands and face and brushed his hair, and, after switching on the porch light, settled down in the sitting-room with a glass of Scotch and *Così fan tutte* on the record player. Though he knew the plot and what the characters were singing about, he found that following the translated libretto helped his concentration.

She came when he had just put on the second record. He left it playing and went to the door. She was half turned away, shaking her umbrella, and the scarf covering her head hid her hair; so that it was not until she had stepped inside and they faced each other in the hall that he saw who she was. His surprise then was such that his voice lifted involuntarily in a second greeting.

'Oh, *hullo!*'

'Do you know me?'

'You once served me in the Beehive.'

'Did I? You weren't a regular, though, were you?'

'Oh, no. There was just the once while you were there.'

'I'm not there any more now.'

'Ah! That explains it.'

'What?'

'Why I hadn't seen you again.'

'Were you looking?'

Her directness was unexpected. 'I noticed.' He held out his hands. 'I didn't know it had started to rain. Let me hang up your coat.' He took it from her while she unfastened her headsquare, shook her hair free and smoothed the hem of her pastel-pink jumper.

'Come through.'

In the sitting-room he had to indicate twice that she should sit down, while he took the record off the player. She sat on the edge of the deep armchair, ankles crossed as she looked round the room. She had pretty legs, Jordan noticed, and she was probably vain about them because her tights were flatteringly fine and of a better quality than the rest of her clothes.

'They're big, aren't they?' she said.

'Beg pardon.'

'These houses. They're bigger than they look from the outside.'

'You'd soon find your way around. I'll show you, later.' He sat down near her. 'Have you done this kind of work before?'

'Not for other people, no.'

'Well, nobody asks for a diploma in cleaning.'

'No.'

'Just for thoroughness. My wife was very thorough.'

'Did she do it all herself?'

'Oh, no. She had a regular woman.'

'What happened to her?'

'She gave up coming when my wife died. I don't think she liked being in the house on her own.'

'Why? There's nothing strange about it, is there?'

'Oh, no. I think she just liked someone to talk to. Is that the kind of thing that would bother you?'

'If you're here to work, you're here to work.'

'Quite. But it's why I have to ask for references. I'd have to give you a key and the run of the house.'

'Oh, yes. You can't be too careful these days.'

'What's your name, by the way?'

'Audrey Nugent.' She was looking into her handbag.

'Mrs Nugent, is it?'

'It was. I was married once.'

'No children?'

'No. Just as well, as it turned out.' She shrugged. 'I picked a wrong 'un.'

'I'm sorry.'

He took the folded manilla envelope she was holding out to him. 'There's these.'

They were both from publicans she had worked for; one, recently dated, from the landlord of the Beehive.

'You say you're doing evening work now?'

'I'm at the Royal Oak, in Ridley.'

'Didn't you like the Beehive?'

'It was further to travel and only a couple of nights a week. I wanted a bit more than that.'

'Hmm.'

'Was that opera you were playing on your gramophone?'

'Yes. Mozart.'

'I used to like Mario Lanza.'

'A bit before your time, surely.'

'I was only a kid. I had some of his records, though. He got fat.'

'Oh, yes?'

'It just piled on to him at the back end. He got like a barrel. Have you got any of his stuff?'

'I'm afraid I haven't.'

'They all seem to get that kind of weight, the best singers. Look at Harry Secombe.'

'And Pavarotti.'

She frowned. 'I don't think I know him.'

'You'll have seen him on television, perhaps.'

'I don't get to see much TV, working nights.'

'No.'

She gave a sudden sigh, more like a catch of breath, clasping

her fingers in her lap, then examining the nails of one hand.
'Are they all right?'

'The references? You seem to have given satisfaction.'

He didn't know. Employers sometimes gave a reference
to get rid of someone. It was hard to refuse anyone who had
not been downright dishonest. Whoever came to him without a personal recommendation he would have to take on
trust. Was she the one? She seemed more subdued now than
when she had arrived, different altogether here from what
he thought of as her natural surroundings, in the lounge
bar of the Beehive, at ease, efficient, chatting with the
regulars, flashing on that smile which had so enchanted
him.

He realised that neither of them had spoken for several
moments and that he was staring at her. He wondered what he
could say to make her smile. He shifted in his chair.

'Would you like to look over the house?'

'If you like.'

'You're still interested . . .?'

'I need the work,' she said bluntly. 'I can't make enough
behind a bar at night. I was a machinist in ready-made clo-
thing,' she went on, 'but everybody's cut back. It's all this
cheap stuff coming in from abroad. They work for nothing
there. It's not as if we were rolling in it.'

Jordan stood up. 'Come and look round.'

She followed him through the house.

'Of course, I don't use all these rooms now.'

'No.'

'But I like the privacy.' Not the loneliness, though, he
thought. Not that.

The choice was his. He would have to decide soon.

'What were you thinking of paying?' she asked as they came
back down the stairs.

He told her, having added a little to what he had found out
was the going rate.

'How many hours?'

'Say three hours, two mornings a week. That should keep
things spick and span.'

'You'd have to take my time-keeping on trust, wouldn't
you?'

'My wife was very fussy,' Jordan said. 'She had a time-clock installed in the hall cupboard.'

Now she laughed. She put her head back and her lips drew away over her teeth, a thin skein of saliva snapping at one corner of her mouth.

He smiled with her. He felt committed now. He asked her if she would come for the first time on a Saturday morning so that he could show her where everything was.

It was as she was putting on her coat that he sensed an uneasiness in her.

'Is anything wrong?'

'I don't like to ask you, but it's dark outside and there's this maniac about. I wonder if you'd be good enough to see me to the bus stop.'

'If you're nervous, I'll drive you home.'

'Oh, no, no.'

'You're quite right to take care. There's no knowing where he might pop up next.'

'I'll be all right at the other end.' He went for his coat. 'I'm not usually timid, but you don't know what it's like to be a woman with him about. You begin to look sideways at every man who comes near you.'

'There's one thing you can be sure of,' Jordan said. 'He isn't coloured green and he hasn't got two heads.'

'What d'you mean?'

'I mean, he'll look like a million other men. Like me, for instance.'

'Give over,' she said.

'Sorry.' Jordan opened the door. 'Is it still raining? I'd better have a hat in any case.'

Her bus went from the other side of the main road. He saw her across and stood with her at the stop.

'I'll be all right now.'

'I'd rather see you safely on.'

'You can call for a quick one.' She nodded at the lighted windows of the Beehive, opposite.

He thought of asking her if she would like a drink before she went, but said instead, 'What's the pub like where you work now?'

'Different.'

There was a double-decker bus standing in a line of traffic at the lights. It swung towards them and pulled up.

'I'll see you Saturday,' she said, stepping on.

'Yes,' Jordan said. 'Saturday.'

One morning several weeks later he had to get out of bed to let her into the house.

'I'd forgotten about the bolt,' he apologised.

'I wondered, when me key wouldn't open it.' She looked at him as he stood in the hall, in his pyjamas and dressing-gown. 'Did you sleep in, or are you – ?'

'I'm not very well,' Jordan said. 'I think I may have the flu.'

It had started yesterday, with a prickling sensation in the soft flesh behind the roof of his mouth. In the afternoon he had begun to sneeze. By evening, his bones were aching and he could not keep warm. He had been sweating in the night and now his pyjamas felt clammy against his skin.

'You get back to bed, out of these draughts,' Mrs Nugent said.

'I must just phone the office.'

She was carrying the vacuum cleaner and dusters from the cupboard under the stairs as he finished his call.

'Don't hang about here. Go back where it's warm. Shall I get you some breakfast?'

'A cup of tea would be welcome.'

'You get off up. I'll bring it in a minute.'

He had not seen her since that first Saturday morning. Every Thursday he left her money in an envelope on the hall table. The house shone and was fragrant with the smell of polish.

'Have you taken anything for it?' she asked when she brought in the tray. 'Can I fetch you anything from the shops?'

He dozed, hearing the whine of the cleaner from downstairs. He was not aware that he had fallen asleep until he woke to find her standing there again.

'How are you feeling now? Is your head thick?'

'No.' He could breathe quite freely.

'Perhaps it's not ready to come out yet. Perhaps it's only a chill.' She put her hand on his forehead in a movement that was totally without diffidence, as though she were a nurse, or

someone who had known him a long time. It was cool and dry.
He wanted her to leave it there. 'You don't feel to have a fever.'

'I really felt quite dreadful last night.'

'A night's sleep and a good sweat. They can work wonders.'

She sat down on the edge of the bed. He felt the pressure of ·
her buttocks against his leg. Jordan had to remind himself that
he had seen her only three times. It was as though the time she
spent alone in the house had given her a familiarity with him.
Yet her voice remained level and impersonal.

'I expect you usually have your lunch out.'

'Yes.'

'What will you do today?'

'I hadn't thought about it.'

'What if I stopped on a while and got you something ready?'

'Oh, no, there's no need for that.'

'I'm not in any rush to get away.'

'I don't know what you'd find.'

'There's bacon and eggs in the fridge. You must eat,
y'know.'

'Yes. Perhaps I will, later.'

She looked at him contemplatively, like someone about to
make a diagnosis or recommend a course of treatment.

'I'll tell you what you ought to do.'

'Mmm?'

'You ought to get up and have a hot shower and get dressed
in some warm clothes. Then come downstairs and have some
bacon and egg.'

Jordan smiled. 'If you say so.'

She nodded and got up. 'I do.'

When, some time later, he was sitting at the kitchen table
with a plate of egg and bacon and fried bread before him,
Jordan said, 'Don't you want anything yourself?'

'Well, I . . .'

'You must have something. You can't stay behind to feed
me and miss your own lunch.'

'All right, then.'

He was finished and drinking a second cup of tea by the time
she sat down opposite him.

'You made short work of that.'

He had eaten with a good appetite. Odd, he thought, how

different the same food could taste when somebody else had cooked it.

'I hope you're settled,' Jordan said. 'Happy in your work,' he explained as she looked at him.

'Oh, yes. It's easy now I'm on top of it. There's nobody to make much of a mess.'

'No.'

'I was thinking I'd wash some of your paintwork down.'

'Whatever you think.'

'Who does your washing for you?'

'You mean my clothes? I've been sending them to a laundry.'

'I didn't know there were any left. That must cost a bomb nowadays.'

'It's not cheap, but – '

'I don't suppose you've all that much. You could put a bundle through the launderette once a week and leave 'em out for me to iron.'

'If you're sure you don't mind.'

An idea came to him. He was silent for a time, not knowing how best to express it.

'I still have all my wife's clothes.'

'Oh?'

'She was about the same build as you.'

'Oh, yes?'

'I don't want to offend you, but she had some nice things. If there was anything you fancied . . .'

'What made you keep them?'

'I've just never bothered about them. I did wonder if I might donate them to an Oxfam shop.'

'Hadn't she any friends who might fancy something?'

'I've lost touch. Besides, some people don't like to – ' He stopped.

'Wear a dead person's clothes, you mean?'

'Perhaps not somebody they've known.'

'I couldn't entertain anything intimate myself.'

'Oh, no, no, no,' Jordan said. 'I could put all that out for jumble. But why don't you look at the rest?'

'All right.'

'Come upstairs,' Jordan said. 'I'll show you what there is.'

A few minutes later he was taking suits and coats out of the fitted wardrobes in his wife's room and laying them on the bed. To them, he added woollens from the tallboy.

'Of course,' he said, 'they might not be your style, but it would be a pity to let anything go that you could make use of.'

'There's some nice things,' she said. She was looking at the labels in the garments. 'Things I could never afford.'

'She was particular,' Jordan said. 'She always went to good shops. But, as I say, please don't be offended, and don't think you'll offend me. It was just an idea.'

She was holding a wool frock against her. It was maroon, with a belt. 'What was her colouring? Was she fair or dark?'

'Fair-skinned. Her hair was sort of nondescript. Mousy, I suppose you'd call it.'

'Like mine when I don't do anything with it.'

'Why do you do things with it?'

'I dunno. Makes a change. D'you think it looks common?'

'Oh, please . . .' Jordan said. 'I didn't mean to be personal.'

'Go on,' she said, 'say what you think.'

'Well, perhaps you could use a rinse or something to bring out its natural colour, without . . . without going so far.'

'Perhaps I could.' She had picked up another frock and was looking into the glass. 'Maybe I will.'

'What do you think, then?' Jordan asked. 'About the clothes.'

'Could I try some of them on?'

'Help yourself. I'll leave you.'

He wandered into his own room where he stood looking aimlessly round before pulling down the duvet and spreading it to air over the foot of his bed. Downstairs in the kitchen, he put on coffee, then, running hot water into the sink, he began to wash the pots they had used. He was standing there with his back to the door when he heard her come in.

'You should have left them to me.'

'I'm not altogether helpless,' Jordan said. 'And you're on overtime already.'

He had switched on the ceiling light which hung low over the table and as he glanced up the darkening window gave him her reflection. For an astounding second he was convinced that it was his wife standing there.

'What do you reckon, then?' she asked as he turned.

She had on the maroon frock, but over it she was wearing his wife's fur cape that she must have gone into another compartment of the wardrobe to find. She seemed suddenly unsure how he would react to this.

'Splendid,' Jordan said.

His stomach churned with a sudden desire to touch her. Looking away, he reached for a towel and dried his hands.

' 'Course, I know you didn't mean this, but I couldn't resist just trying it on.' Her hands were stroking the fur in long soft movements.

'Why not?' Jordan heard himself saying. Then, when he realised she did not understand: 'Why shouldn't I have meant that as well?'

'You can't,' she said, lifting her gaze to his. 'It must be worth a small fortune.'

'Not all that much,' Jordan said. 'And so what?'

'You can re-sell furs like this,' she said. 'Don't shops take 'em back?'

'I don't want to sell it.'

'You can't give it to me, though. I couldn't take it.'

'Why not? I bought it. Why shouldn't I give it to whom I like?'

'You'll want it for a lady friend.'

'I haven't got one.'

'You will have. You'll want to get married again, some time. Won't you?' she said after a moment, all the time her fingers moving along the lie of the fur. 'What is it, anyway?'

'Blue fox, I think,' Jordan said. 'Yes, blue fox.'

'It's beautiful.'

'Won't you let me give it to you?'

'Hang on a tick,' she said on a slight laugh. 'I'm just your cleaning woman. You don't hardly know me.'

'I don't want to embarrass you . . .'

'You are, though.'

'Sorry.'

'I'll have to think about it.'

'Was there anything else you fancied?'

'I'll take this frock. There's one or two other things I like.'

'Take anything you want,' Jordan said. 'And think about the coat. It will still be there when you've made up your mind.'

She had taken off the cape and was standing with it over her arm, her free hand still moving in long strokes across the fur.

'I ought to be going, before it gets dark.'

'I've kept you late. I'll put it on your wages on Thursday.'

She laughed. 'Nay, I reckon I've been paid enough.'

'Would you like me to drive you home?'

'You stop in and keep warm. How are you feeling now?'

Jordan put the back of his hand to his forehead. 'I don't really know.'

'You get a few whiskies inside you and have an early night. You'll likely feel better tomorrow.'

He sat for a long time at the kitchen table after she had gone, while the light faded in the sky beyond the garden. She had left in a casual, almost offhand manner which had taken him by surprise after the near-intimacy of their talk about the clothes. 'I'll be off, then,' she had said, and before he could stir himself from the reverie in which he was peeling the maroon frock off her shoulders and freeing her breasts for the touch of his hands, the front door had closed behind her. He told himself that he had made her uneasy; that she lacked the social grace to handle the situation he had created. She would brood about its implications, wondering what his generosity implied, and – never crediting its spontaneity – from now on keep up her guard. Not that any of it really mattered, for they would not meet again unless he contrived it.

He asked himself if he could justify taking two more days off work so that he could be here when she came again, on Thursday. Could he risk scaring her off altogether by doing that? But he must, he told himself, build now on what had been started – on that curious apparently disinterested familiarity with which she had felt his temperature and sat on his bed; the way they had looked at his wife's clothes together; her coming down in the fur cape. Why had she done that if she had not coveted it and wanted to give him a chance to offer it to her?

At first he drank one cup of coffee after another, telling himself that if he did not move he could pretend that she was still in the house, moving about those empty rooms. Then he

got up to fetch whisky and as he was coming back through the
hall the telephone rang.

It was his secretary. He had not spoken to her earlier, but left
a message in her absence. Now she asked how he was and if he
thought he would be well enough to keep an appointment he
had made for Thursday morning with the representatives of
the unions.

Jordan's firm enjoyed good industrial relations, but in-
creasingly sophisticated technology entailed keeping the
unions sweetened. It was vital always that nothing should go
by default.

'If I feel like I do now,' he told Mrs Perrins, 'I'll be in at the
usual time tomorrow.'

The first thing he noticed when he came into the house after
work on Thursday was her envelope lying on the hall table.
With her wages he had slipped in a note saying, 'Do please
think seriously about the coat.'

Wondering why she had not telephoned, it occurred to him
that she probably did not know his office number. Perhaps she
would ring this evening. Perhaps, on the other hand, she was
ill and could not leave the house.

It came to him now how little he knew about her. He had
never made a note of the address she had given him and his
only clue to where she could be found was the name of the pub
where she had said she was working. It took him a few
minutes, while he poured himself a drink and began preparing
his evening meal, to bring that to mind.

He looked it up in the yellow pages, then got out a street
map of the city and its suburbs. He did not like to think of her
being short of money over the weekend, nor of the possibility
that she was too ill to get out to the shops.

There had been no call from her by mid-evening, when he
got his car out again and drove across the city. The Royal Oak
was a big, square, late Victorian pub with two floors of letting
rooms above the tall windows of the public rooms on the
ground floor. Its best days had obviously finished when
commercial travellers abandoned the train for the motor car
and no longer spent three or four nights in one place. Now its

badly lighted and greasily carpeted bars served as a local for the occupants of the score of streets of three-storey redbrick terraces which climbed the hill beside the main road – and, Jordan thought, only the seediest of them. He detested everything about the place, from the smell of stale beer and the garish wallpaper to the few people he could see – the lads in motorbike gear round the pool table under the wall-mounted television set; the shabby, earnestly gesticulating men drinking in the passage by the back entrance; and the shirtsleeved landlord who put his cigarette on the rim of an already full ashtray before coming to serve him. Jordan wondered when trade here justified Mrs Nugent's wages. He ordered a Scotch and looked with distaste at the glass it came in.

'Does Mrs Nugent work here?' he asked when the man brought his change.

'Audrey?'

'Yes. Is she on tonight?'

'She should be, but she sent word she was poorly.'

'Does she live nearby?'

'Are you looking for her?'

'I'm a friend of hers from when she worked at the Beehive.'

The landlord had taken in his clothes and now an expression Jordan couldn't read flickered briefly in his pale eyes.

'She lives in Birtmore Street.'

'Where's that?'

'Second on your left going back towards town. I couldn't tell you what number. Happen the wife'd know.'

'I'd be grateful if you'd ask her.'

'You're sure you're not after her for something else?'

'I don't follow you,' Jordan said. Perhaps the publican did not know that Mrs Nugent had another job. How did Jordan know what compartments she chose to divide her life into? He had told the man enough of his business.

'Some folk round here, y'know,' the landlord said, 'they're no better than they ought to be.'

'I'm only enquiring about Mrs Nugent,' Jordan said. 'I'm not interested in anybody else.'

Jordan sipped his whisky. The man nodded at the glass as he put it down. 'Same again?'

Jordan looked. There was still some left. 'Go on, then.'

The man went away, taking the glass, and spoke into a house phone.

'She'll be down in a minute.'

'There doesn't seem to be enough work for a barmaid,' Jordan said.

'That's where you're wrong. We get the young 'uns in disco nights.'

'Is that the kind of thing you enjoy yourself?'

'Times is bad. You've got to move with 'em. When Audrey and the missus are on together, I get in the public bar and leave 'em to it.'

He went to serve a youth in a studded leather jacket whose head was shaved to the bone up to the crown, where the hair sprayed out in lacquered vermilion fronds. When a woman with wispy fair hair, wearing a yellow hand-knitted jumper with short puffed-out sleeves appeared, she spoke to the man, who nodded his head in Jordan's direction.

'Audrey, was it, you was asking about?'

'I'd be grateful if you'd give me her address.'

'From the social security, are you?'

'I'd have her address if I were, wouldn't I?'

'Does she know you're coming?'

'I thought I'd see her here.'

'You would have in the normal way, but she's poorly.'

'So your husband says. He says she lives in Birtmore Street. What number is it?'

'Twenty-seven.' She looked at him as though regretting the ready answer.

Jordan left the premises wondering if everyone who frequented them had things to hide. It depressed him to think of Audrey Nugent spending her evenings there, and depressed him yet more to reflect that she had probably more in common with that place and its clientele than she had with the Beehive, and even more so than with him himself.

He sat in his car for several minutes before starting the engine and considered the wisdom of what he'd set out to do. Would she welcome his visit or think he was prying? He did not, he admitted now, seriously think she was in need of the money – not in urgent need, or she would have taken steps to get it. Now that he knew her address, he could put it in the post. Yet if he turned back now he would only castigate himself for his indecisiveness. 'Be honest,' he said out loud. 'Own up. You've come because you want to see her.'

He drove in second gear back along the main road and turned up the hill when his headlights picked out the cracked nameplate on a garden wall. Some of the houses had been fitted with incongruous new doors and windows. Others showed neglect in broken gates and leggy, overgrown privet hiding the small squares of soil that passed for front gardens. One such was number twenty-seven, which Jordan found when he had traversed the length of the street and kerb-crawled half-way down again. A dormer window had been let into the roof of this house and a dim light showed through the frosted-glass upper panels of the front door.

The money was in his pocket, still sealed in the envelope he had left for her with her name on it. All he need do was slip it through the letterbox. Then, he thought, she might, in that occasional direct way of hers, rebuke him later. 'Why didn't you knock? What were you scared of? Coming all that way and going away without knocking and having a word.'

He got out of the car and approached the house, still undecided. He was standing there with the envelope in his hand when a shape loomed up between the source of the light and the door, and the door was suddenly flung open wide before him. A man coming out at speed stopped in his tracks as Jordan stepped back to avoid being shouldered aside.

'Are you looking for somebody?'

'I believe Mrs Nugent lives here.'

The man grunted, his glance raking Jordan in a quick appraisal. 'Number three, first floor back.' He half turned and bawled up the stairs. 'Audrey! Bloke to see you,' then plunged out past Jordan, leaving him facing an empty hallway, with an image of a strongly built man in his middle thirties, with close dark curly hair, a dark polo-neck sweater and a tweed jacket which Jordan, for some reason, was convinced had been handed on or picked up secondhand.

He stepped into the hall and closed the door as a woman's voice called from above. 'Who is it?' He hesitated to call back and began to mount the stairs, hearing as he went up the creak of boards on the landing. 'Are you still there, Harry?' the voice asked. The woman's head and shoulders appeared over the rail and as she saw Jordan's shape she said sharply, her voice rising, 'Who are you? What d'you want?'

'It's all right, Mrs Nugent. It's only me – Mr Jordan.'

She straightened up and stepped back as he reached the landing and light fell on him from the open door of the room behind her.

'What the heck are *you* doing here?'

Her question was almost insolent in its phrasing and abruptness. He would have reprimanded anyone at the works who spoke to him like that. But she was on her home ground: he was the intruder, and he had startled her.

'I'm sorry,' Jordan said. 'I came to bring your money and ask if you're all right.'

'Oh, that could have waited.'

'And when there was no word . . .'

She had backed into the doorway of her room and was standing with a hand on either jamb, as though denying him entrance, or – it suddenly struck him – looking, in the creased, floor-length plum-coloured housecoat, its neck cut in a deep V to a high tight elasticated waist which clung to her ribcage under her breasts, like a still from a Hollywood *film noir* of the 1940s.

'You took a bit of finding,' Jordan said, and wondered at his exaggeration. Perhaps it was all of a piece with his new image of her as the *femme fatale* of a Fritz Lang movie.

'How's that?'

'I had to enquire at the pub.'

'The Royal Oak, y'mean?'

'Yes. I hope you don't mind. They seemed a bit . . . a bit cagey.'

'They wouldn't know who you were.'

'No.'

'Did you tell 'em?'

'No. I didn't think it was any of their business.'

'You're right, it isn't.'

Jordan held out the envelope. 'The money's here, just as I left it for you. You might need it if you've lost your wages at the pub as well.'

'Thanks. You're very thoughtful.' Taking the envelope, she

lifted both hands to rub at her upper arms. 'There's a rare draught coming up them stairs. Didn't you shut the front door?'

'Yes, I'm sure I did.' He went to the top of the stairs and looked down. 'Yes, I did.' He glanced back at her. 'Well, I hope you'll soon feel better. Can I expect you on Tuesday? I mean, don't worry if you're still not up to it.'

'Don't you want to come in a minute?'

'I mustn't disturb you.'

'Come in, if you want. I'll warn you, though, it's a tip. I haven't cleaned up today.'

Jordan followed her into the room. A sink, electric cooker and a small fridge occupied a curtained-off corner. She cleared some garments and magazines off the seat of a wooden-armed easy-chair. 'Sit down.' She went and sat on the edge of a divan whose covers were crumpled as though she had been lying on it. 'See how the other three-quarters live,' she said. 'Cosy, isn't it?' There was a sardonic glint in her eyes as she looked at him.

'Is this all you have, just the one room?'

'That's all.'

'You rent it furnished?'

'If you can call this junk furniture.'

Jordan's was the only chair. He wondered where the man he had met at the door had sat, if he had been in the room.

Mrs Nugent was tearing open the envelope. As Jordan remembered that his note about the fur coat was still in there, she took it out, glanced at it and replaced it with the banknotes, without comment.

'*You* seem nicely back on your feet, anyway.'

'I had a couple of important meetings. It seemed to leave me as quickly as it came. I hope you didn't catch it from me.'

'No, mine's a woman's ailment. I wait every month, wondering if it'll be a bad one. When it is, it crucifies me. Fair cuts me in two. No wonder they call it the curse.'

'Surely nowdays there are things . . .'

'I was fine while I was on the pill. But then they began to get windy about keeping women on it too long.' She shrugged. 'So now it's back to codeine and cups of tea.'

'The chap I bumped into,' Jordan said, 'is he a fellow tenant?'

'My step-brother. He comes and goes. Works away a lot.

Oil rigs and suchlike. Sometimes abroad, among the Arabs.'
She got up. 'He brought some whisky. Would you like some?'
There was a half-bottle of Johnny Walker on the draining
board.

'Well, I . . .'

She was rinsing a tumbler under the tap. 'Have a drink. You
like whisky, don't you?'

'Just a small one, then,' Jordan said. 'I had a couple in the
pub.'

'Another one won't get you into trouble.'

He asked for water and she handed the drink to him, half and
half.

'Cheers, then.'

'All the best.'

'And thanks for coming over with the money.'

'I had visions of you laid up without any.'

'I wonder you've no more to think about than me. Do you
look after all your people that way?'

'I try to see they get a fair deal. But I have staff for that.'

'Are there any jobs going at your place?'

'I'm afraid not. We've enough on finding work for those we
have. Perhaps when things pick up.'

'If they ever do.' She drank, her face suddenly sombre.
Jordan wondered if she ever allowed herself to think about the
future, or simply lived from day to day.

'Could I ask you,' he said, 'if it's not too personal. But do
you manage to make ends meet?'

'Look at this place,' she said, 'and work it out for yourself.'

After the chill of the night outside and the draughty stairs,
the heat in the room was beginning to make Jordan's head
swim. An electric fire blazed at full a few feet from his legs. He
would, he thought, have to take off his overcoat or leave.
About, for the moment, to shift the chair back for fear of
scorching his trousers, he paused in his movement and relaxed
his weight as the orange glow of the fire's elements suddenly
faded to a dull red, then to black.

'Blast!' Audrey Nugent said. She reached for a purse and
poked her forefinger into its pockets. Then she got up and
looked on the narrow mantelshelf.

'Is it on a meter?' Jordan asked.

'You bet it's on a meter. He could nearly let you live rent-free, the profit he makes on that.'

'Let me . . .' Jordan took change out of his pocket and counted out half a dozen tenpence pieces. 'Here . . .'

'If you can make it up to the pound, I'll give you a note for it.'

'There's not enough,' Jordan said. 'It doesn't matter.'

She knelt by the sink and fed coins into the meter. 'Lucky you came.'

As the fire began to glow again, Jordan said, 'I wonder you can breathe in such heat.'

'Happen you're right. I do overdo it a bit when I'm not feeling well.' She switched off one of the bars, then drew on a woollen cardigan over the housecoat. At once all the presence – the allure, even – bestowed by the coat was gone. 'I was going to make meself a hot drink and get into bed, anyway.'

'I'm being a nuisance,' Jordan said.

'You walk on eggshells trying not to offend people, don't you?'

'Not everybody,' Jordan said. 'Not by any means.'

'What's so special about me, then?'

'You're in my private employ,' Jordan said, and wondered what other, less pompous form of words he could have used.

She drew the cardigan together across her chest and fastened the top buttons. Then she felt about in the crumpled folds of the divan cover until she found a cigarette packet, which she shook before tossing it towards a wastebox by the sink.

'You wouldn't have a cigarette on you?'

'I don't smoke,' Jordan said. 'I'll go and get you some, if you like.'

'Don't bother. Harry 'ull bring some back with him, if he remembers.'

'He's coming back?'

'He's kipping down here for the time being.'

'Oh . . .' Despite himself, Jordan let his gaze take in once more the limits of the room. 'You mean . . .?'

'I mean in here. That's his sleeping-bag on the floor behind your chair. It's just till he finds a place of his own, or takes his hook again. It won't be for long. He says it won't, anyway.' She shrugged. 'It helps with the expenses.'

Letting his imagination run free, Jordan had been rehearsing in it an exchange in which he offered to pay her rent for the privilege of visiting her one evening a week and making love to her on that narrow divan. Only an idle fantasy, he told himself. But he was sick of cold women with pretensions; he wanted someone direct, earthy, warm. He tried to imagine her response should he venture the suggestion, and saw her laughing in his face before ordering him out.

An alternative began to form – one more drastic in its way, but an offer she could refuse without offence, while leaving him with room for further manoeuvre. While he was turning it over, wondering if now was the right time to put it to her, she got up with a restless movement and taking the whisky bottle held it out to him without speaking, her hips moving inside the housecoat as she shifted her weight from one leg to the other, like one waiting for some overdue event.

She probably wanted him to go, he thought, as he shook his head and she carelessly slopped another half-inch into her own glass; wondering why he was hanging about now that his errand was done. Yet although this single cluttered room with its cheap tat of fittings and furniture oppressed him, he was held by the intimacy of their being alone here. The material of the housecoat – some kind of thin stretch velvet, he thought – hugged her hips in a clean slim line, and as she sat again its weight settled into the V of her thighs at the bottom of her flat belly. She carried no spare weight and her breasts would be small, small and firm and white, high on her long white body.

'Aren't you sweltering in that overcoat?' she asked suddenly, when neither of them had spoken for a time.

Jordan realised how long his silence had been and that this might have brought on the nervous energy of her movements.

'I must go,' he said. 'I've taken up too much of your time.'

'You're not spoiling anything. But I wondered why you'd turned so broody.'

'I'm sorry,' Jordan said, 'but I – '

'I've never heard anybody apologise so much. What d'you think you've done?'

'Made you slightly uneasy, perhaps. I don't know you well enough to go quiet in your company like that.'

'Be my guest,' she said. 'Was it something important?'

'Yes,' Jordan heard himself admitting, and knew that he must now carry the thought through. 'I was just weighing the pros and cons of – '

'The what?'

He was thrown for a moment. 'I don't understand.'

'It's me that doesn't understand you. The prose and . . . what did you say?'

'Things for, things against,' Jordan said.

'For and against what?'

'Asking you to come and be my housekeeper.'

It silenced her. She looked quickly at him and just as quickly away. A small smile touched her lips – whether of amusement, embarrassment or gratification he could not tell.

'If you'll just let me explain,' he went on.

'I think you'd better.'

Jordan was struck by the panicky thought that the step-brother might return before he could say it all.

'The house needs a woman in it,' he said. 'I mean, more than you can give it by just coming in twice a week. And I'm tired of cooking for myself. If it comes to that, I don't like living on my own there, either. There's plenty of room. You could easily – '

'You are talking about living in, then?'

'Oh, yes,' Jordan said. It was not, in fact, what he'd immediately had in mind, but the idea had grown as he was talking. 'You could have your own, er, quarters. I could easily make one of the upstairs rooms into a bedsitter. But other than that you'd have the run of the place and be perfectly free to do what you liked with your spare time. You could carry on working in the evenings if you felt you needed the change and the company. You might think that what I could offer you wasn't a full wage. I'm sure we could work something out, though, and you would have a comfortable home and all found.'

'Wait a minute,' she said as he stopped talking. 'Hold on a tick. This is all a bit fast for me. It wants some thinking about.'

'You don't have to decide now.'

'No. It's just as well.'

She had clenched the fingers of one hand and was pushing the fist deep into her abdomen. The sudden pallor of her face perturbed Jordan.

'Is there anything I can get you, Mrs Nugent?'

'It'll go,' she said. 'That's the only good thing about it.'

Jordan got up. 'We'll talk about it another time, when you can put your mind to it.'

'You're a fast worker, I'll say that for you.'

'Please,' Jordan said, 'don't get me wrong.'

'I mean, you know next to nothing about me.'

'Nor you me, if it comes to that.'

'Haven't you thought what a risk you'd be taking?'

He had. Yet he also knew that a desire to do something for this woman had been growing in him ever since she had first smiled at him, in the Beehive. Why, if she would only let him, he could transform her life: he could take her out of this squalor, put her into decent clothes, give her a security that picking up part-time work where she could had never offered her. He would become her benefactor, friend, protector. Gradually, she would learn that she had someone of substance to turn to.

He held in his excitement at the prospect and curbed the urge to press his offer now, though the spasm of pain seemed to have left her as she drew herself upright, arching her back and taking a deep breath which she let out in a long sigh.

'What if it didn't work out?' she said. 'Where would I go then?'

'Why not come for a week or two first?' Jordan suggested. 'Keep this place on in the meantime. Let your step-brother look after it.'

'When would you want to know?'

'There's no hurry,' Jordan said. 'Don't bother about it now. Think it over when you're well again.'

On his way home Jordan was stopped by the police, who had put a barrier across the suburban road he had chosen on no more than a whim. They did not tell him what they were looking for, only that they were on a routine check, before they asked him who he was, where he lived, where he had been and how long he had been away from home. Then they requested permission to shine their torches over the interior of his car and to examine the contents of the boot.

Jordan guessed what had happened and the local news on his alarm-radio woke him next morning with the details. A girl had been done to death only two hundred yards from a busy main road. It seemed that she had been found more quickly than some of the others and that she must have died while he was talking to Mrs Nugent. There were no details of how the killing had been carried out, but there were the usual hints of appalling savagery. Women were once again warned not to go out alone after dark: the attacks were no longer confined to one type of woman and all women should now consider themselves at risk.

During the next few days he found himself fretting about Audrey Nugent's safety. True, she had her step-brother at hand, but Jordan did not know how responsible he was; and Mrs Nugent herself, though sometimes anxious, was unlikely to let her movements be restricted.

He wanted to go and see her again, to reassure himself and to warn her. But he dared not seem to be pestering. It was best that she be left to get used gradually to the idea he had planted. So he spent a restless weekend that only hardened the conviction that he was planning the right course for him, and contented himself by leaving a note for her on the Tuesday morning, which did not refer to his offer, but merely said, 'Do please take care when you are out.'

He returned from the works in the early evening and let himself into the house, his pulse suddenly racing as he saw the light in the kitchen and knew she was still there. He made no effort to keep the pleasure out of his voice as she came out to meet him.

'Hullo! Have you been here all day?'

'I came after dinner. Thought I'd stop on a bit.'

'I *am* glad. You've no idea how good it is to come home and find someone in the house.'

'Have you never lived on your own before?'

'As a young man, yes. I lived in a flat for a while. But that was different.'

'I expect you still miss your wife.'

He said, 'I miss her not being here. We were married for a long time. You get used to things. Even things you don't especially care for at the time.'

She frowned a little, turning that over, until she realised that he was frowning too as he looked at her, or at the clothes she was wearing under her pinafore: a skirt and fawn jumper, sleeves pushed to the elbows, that he vaguely recognised.

'I found something else that fit me. I hope you don't mind.'

'Fine,' he said. 'Didn't I tell you? I couldn't quite bring them to mind. There were some things she stopped wearing when she put on a bit of weight. As long as you don't find them too conservative.'

'Conservative?'

'Plain. A bit dull.'

'Oh, I sometimes think I'm a bit too tempted by bright colours, myself. I like folk to see me coming.'

'You must trust your own taste in things.'

'All the same, you could mebbe pull me up when you think I'm going too far.'

Jordan was delighted. 'Would you let me do that? Wouldn't you mind? Really?'

'You're a gentleman. You don't want a housekeeper who looks like – well, a barmaid from the Royal Oak.'

He could hardly believe what she was saying. 'Does that mean you're coming? Have you made up your mind?'

'You said something about giving it a try. Me bag's upstairs. I thought I'd stop for a day or two and see how it works out.'

At the end of each working day, Jordan sat for a few minutes after clearing his desk and basked in the pleasure of knowing she would be there when he got home. They would have a glass of sherry then, his the *fino*, hers something rather sweeter, and discuss their evening meal. She was a competent plain cook and all he had to do was unobtrusively add the spices and herbs whose uses she seemed unaware of. She remarked on their flavour with approval.

'You seem to do all right by yourself. I don't know what you need me for.'

'There's a difference between helping and doing it all the time.'

'I was wondering about your shopping.' They had so far used food from his freezer.

'Do you want to do it?'

'If you tell me what to get and how much to spend. You'll have to see to the fancier things yourself.'

'Perhaps we could do it together to start with.'

'If you like.'

'When, though? When could we fit it in?'

'What about Saturday morning?'

'That's all right by me, but –'

'You don't work then, do you, or go playing golf?'

Jordan laughed. 'Whatever made you think about golf?'

'I just thought you might play.'

'I did try it once,' Jordan said, 'but I couldn't take to it. No, Saturday's all right, but what about your weekend?'

'What about it?'

'Do you mean you're staying over?'

'If you want me to.'

'What about your job at the pub?'

'I told 'em I was going away for a few days. I'll mebbe pack it in altogether if things turn out right here.'

'I hope they will.'

'You're satisfied with it so far?'

'So far,' Jordan said, smiling.

His greatest fear was that, alone all day, she would become bored and begin to pine for the old life: the lights, the noise of crowded places, the kind of company she had been used to.

'You mustn't think you've got to stay in all the time,' he told her. 'Just be careful not to be alone on the streets after dark.'

'I'm all right,' she said, 'for now. I'm enjoying the change.'

She liked to bathe before she went to bed; he, in the morning. He wondered how often she had bathed before and suspected that it was not every day. But now each evening she made the most of the privacy of the bathroom, the huge soft unused towels he had got out for her and the abundant hot water. Going in after her, he would brush his teeth standing in the humid scent of bath oil and talcum powder and think of her long slim body lying in one of the two single beds in the guest room she had chosen to sleep in. Each morning, as his radio switched on, she brought him a cup of tea and quietly informed him that breakfast would be ready in fifteen minutes.

He had not asked for this and was startled by her first appearance at his bedside in the plum-coloured housecoat he had seen her in before, though she performed the service in the same matter-of-fact way in which she had put her hand to his forehead when he was not well, and she was out of the room again before he had lifted himself on to his elbow. In everything it was as if she were striving to do exactly what he expected of her; in all but the smallest, most routine matters she waited for his cue. He, in turn, longed for a familiarity in which he would know instinctively how to please her, while savouring the novelty, the strangeness of her presence in the house.

On Saturday morning Jordan and Mrs Nugent moved slowly along the aisles of the best of the nearby supermarkets, he choosing articles from the shelves while she pushed the trolley beside him. His wife had loathed supermarkets and had patronised a number of local shops, where she was known by name and could ask for precisely what she wanted, and, in some cases, have it delivered.

'What shall we have for dinner tonight? There's tomorrow as well, isn't there? Are you fond of steak? Do you think as there are two of us we could run to a small joint? If there's anything left we can eat it cold – or I can – in the week. What kind of vegetable do you like best? No, you say; I really don't mind: brussels sprouts, cauliflower, whatever you fancy. Look, there's some asparagus. We could have it with the steak, or perhaps as a starter. Don't you like it? Oh, you don't know. Well, let's take some; I know you'll enjoy it when you taste it. I quite like fish as a change, too. I have one or two good recipes for fish. But if we want that we shall have to go to the fishmonger down the road.'

They were nearing the checkout when the woman – a friend of his wife's – whom he hadn't noticed, spoke to Jordan.

'Hullo, Robert. You're quite a stranger. Where have you been hiding yourself?'

Mrs Nugent turned her head to look, then moved on a few discreet yards and examined a display of tableware. Jordan made polite noises.

'How are you bearing up? Time does slip by, doesn't it? Henry and I were only speaking about you the other day and

reminding ourselves that we ought to be getting in touch. But
you're not alone, I see. I spotted you from over there, before I
saw your friend. I've got to confess that it gave me something
of a turn.'

'Mrs Nugent helps me in the house.'

'Oh, I see. It was the coat that did it. I caught a back view and
I could have sworn it was just like one that Marjorie wore.'

'Do you really think so?'

'Perhaps I'm wrong. It wouldn't be the first time. Henry
always says I'm just as likely to get hold of the wrong end of
the stick as the right one. But then, *he's* not to be relied on in all
things. You look as though you'll have quite spent up. I expect
you like to get it all done in one fell swoop, instead of popping
out for bits and pieces. That's more a man's way. And it was
such a comfort to Marjorie's friends to know that you could
cope. "Oh, he's quite capable, Robert," I remember telling
someone at the time. "Robert can cope." And of course you
never know just how much people prefer to be left to their
thoughts at such sad times. Some people like to be taken out of
themselves, others to be left alone with their memories. I did
wonder, though, how long you'd be before you put the house
on the market. A lovely house – a real family home – but I
always thought it just a touch big even for the two of you. I
know Marjorie loved it. She told me so once. "I like space to
breathe and room to turn round without falling over Robert,"
she said. Just her joke. You've still got Marjorie's father's
snuff-boxes, I suppose? Henry was talking about them the
other day too. Always admired those. Not that he could afford
to buy them, even if you wanted to sell. They must be worth
thousands . . . Yes . . . poor Marjorie. I do still miss her, you
know. But perhaps I shouldn't say things like that to you when
you've learned to come to terms with it. And if you've got
someone bobbing in and out and helping you to keep things
spick and span – wasn't Marjorie the houseproud one? – you
won't feel so entirely alone. I must say you've been very
fortunate to find somebody. It's so hard to find help nowadays, even with all this unemployment. Reliable help, I mean,
because you can't be too careful who you let over your
doorstep. Did you find her through an agency, or . . .?'

'Recommended by a friend.'

'Oh, well, that's ideal . . . That back view. It gave me quite a moment. Do give us a ring and come round some time. We rarely go out now that Henry's retired, except for the occasional drive. And of course none of us goes out in the dark any more. We daren't. Terrible, terrible. What can the police be doing not to have caught him before this?'

Jordan walked unhurriedly after Mrs Nugent, who had moved out of sight. She turned to him as he rounded the end of the shelves. 'Silly bitch,' he said, and for a second her face retained its thoughtful gravity before breaking into that smile which, rare as it was now, always seemed to him like the sun coming out.

'Did you tell her who I was?'

'Of course. What is there to hide?'

Nothing, Except his thoughts. His occasional reveries. His projections of a future for which he could see no durable shape. 'Live each day as it comes,' he told himself, 'and be grateful for it. Build on whatever we're establishing.' She seemed content and he was happier than he had been in years: conscious of his happiness and trying not to spoil it by fearing that it would not last.

After supper, which they ate together, using the dining-room at her suggestion, and she had washed up, refusing his offer of help, he read for an hour while she watched television in another room. He wanted to join her, but as she respected his privacy so he must respect her free time. Perhaps later, if she stayed, he would hire a video recorder so that she would not be deprived of programmes by her evening chores.

At a little after eleven she looked into the room and said, 'If you don't want the bathroom for a while I'll go up now.'

'Okay. Isn't the late-night film any good?'

'It's foreign, and I'm tired.'

'Bed's the best place, then.'

'By the way, what time do you like breakfast on a Sunday?'

'Any time we both feel like it. I think you could lie in for an hour, if you want to.'

'I'll see. Goodnight, then.'

'Goodnight.'

He put a record of singing on the player and poured himself a Scotch. After a time he went across the hall to the room where she had been sitting to unplug the television set from the mains. The room smelled of cigarette smoke and there were four stubs in the ashtray. He left them. She would, he had no doubt, tidy in here in the morning and open the window briefly for fresh air. Before disconnecting the set he switched on. A man was speaking to a woman in passionate French. She answered him, accusing him of using her for his own devices. Jordan's French was not good enough for him to follow the exchange and a stilted moment in the translation in the subtitles made him suddenly laugh out loud.

Something woke him in the small hours. He lay there, trying to make out what it was. He had no recollection of a dream, yet his heart was racing as if he had surfaced from a nightmare. He turned on to his back and listened to the house as he had listened every night for a time after his wife had died. The feeling of unease persisted. Finally, he gave in to it and switched on his bedside light and threw back the duvet. Pushing his feet into his slippers, he got up and drew on his dressing-room before stepping on to the landing.

He was standing looking over the rail into the darkness below when he heard the sound. It was like the soft, plaintive whimper of some small animal, trapped and bewildered; and it was coming from Mrs Nugent's room. As he moved to the door and put his ear to the panel, the animal-like plaint changed to indistinct words uttered in a rapid, low-pitched stream. When the voice all at once rose in a cadence of defiance, Jordan tapped lightly on the door and opened it. He had to step round the door before he could make out the shape of her lying in the nearer of the twin beds. For a moment then it was as though his presence had soothed her without her knowing it; then one of her arms began to thrash as she spoke again in a vehement outburst:

'No! No! You can't. I won't let you. You can't! You can't! You can't!'

'Mrs Nugent.' As he touched her shoulder, she twisted violently away from him, then back again. 'Mrs Nugent.'

She spoke as if still held in her dream. 'Who is it? What d'you want?'

'It's only me, Mrs Nugent. Don't be alarmed. You were only dreaming.' He knelt beside the bed now, one hand holding her hand that was free of the covers. With his other hand he found himself softly caressing her brow, then her cheek. 'You're all right now. Don't be afraid. You're safe with me.' There were tears on her face. He cupped her cheek and ran his thumb in the moisture under her eyes. She lay still now, allowing herself to be soothed.

Jordan raised himself and sat on the bed. She shifted herself to make room for him as she felt his weight settle. He began again to caress the pale shape of her face. Her hair was damp on her forehead.

'You're quite safe,' Jordan said. 'You're perfectly safe with me. I won't let them hurt you.'

In a few moments more her breathing was steady and deep. He wondered if she had really awakened.

He found her sitting at the kitchen table, drinking tea and smoking a cigarette.

'Good morning.'

'Hullo. You're up early. I thought you were going to sleep in a bit.'

'I forgot to reset my radio. It woke me at the usual time.' He got a cup from the cupboard and reached for the teapot, motioning her to stay seated as she made to rise. 'I can do it.' He nodded towards the thin plume of smoke which rose lazily in the still air beyond the tall creosoted fence of his neighbour's garden. 'It must be going to be a nice day.'

'D'you think so?'

'He always makes a fire on the nicest days.' He joined her at the table. 'I thought you might have slept longer yourself.'

She drew on the cigarette. Her hand trembled slightly as she tapped ash into the glass tray.

'Did you come into my room last night?'

'Don't you remember?'

'Somebody was touching me.'

'You were dreaming. You woke me up.'

'I took a sleeping pill. I didn't know where I was.'

'You were frightened.'

'I must have been.'

'What was it about, can you remember?'

'Not much now.' She frowned. 'I was here on me own. It was different, somehow. Somebody came.'

'Who was it?'

'I don't know.'

'Do you often have nightmares?'

'I dream sometimes, but not like that. I haven't had one like that since I was a little lass. I mean as bad. They used to have to take me into bed between them.'

'Your father and mother?'

'Yes.'

'Were you an only child?'

'Yes.'

'Are they still alive?'

'Me mother died, after me dad ran off. I never heard what happened to him.' Jordan drank tea and waited, saying nothing. 'Do you want some breakfast?'

'There's no hurry.'

'Have *you* got any family?'

'My parents are dead. I have a married sister in New Zealand and a brother living in London.'

'Do you ever see them?'

'My brother came up for my wife's funeral. I hadn't seen him for some time before that.'

'You're not close, then?'

'No.'

'I think that's a shame. I pined for brothers and sisters when I was a kid.'

'You've got your step-brother.'

'Well . . . He's not really me step-brother. I just call him that. It's what he calls himself.'

'I don't follow.'

'Me mam was never married to his dad.'

'You all lived together?'

'For a year or two. Then me mam died. An auntie took me in. I never saw Harry again till we were both grown up. He come looking for me, one time. "Don't you know me?" he says. "It's your step-brother." I didn't know him from Adam at first. Then I begun to see the likeness. He always calls me his step-sister. I don't mind, if that's what he wants. It makes things look a bit more respectable, I suppose, when he turns up and wants a place to sleep for a week or two. Not that that matters much. Nobody cares nowadays, do they?'

'Apparently not.'

'Does it bother *you*, then, that sort of thing?'

'Oh, I always say people can do what they like, as long as they don't do it in the street and frighten the horses.'

'You what?'

'Just an old joke. What did Harry think of you coming to live in here?'

'I don't really know.'

'Didn't he say anything? Did he think it was a good move or a bad one?'

'He said it was up to me.'

'Do you think you can still settle, after last night?'

'Nothing happened last night, did it?'

'You were crying out in your sleep. I came in and calmed you.'

'Was that all?'

'Can't you remember?'

'I must have had another dream, after you'd gone.'

'What about?' Her cup was empty. He reached for the pot and refilled it for her, not wanting her to start moving about. 'What was your other dream, then? You weren't frightened again, were you?'

'No.' She shook her head and lowered her face, one hand to her forehead.

'Do you mean *I* was in it?'

'It's too silly . . .'

'Silly?'

'Embarrassing. It's best not talked about.'

'But you thought it might actually have happened. Is that what you mean?'

'Not really.'

'It was vivid, though. It must have been.'

'I told you, I'd taken a sleeping pill. I didn't know where I was.'

'If it wasn't frightening, was it curious or pleasant, or what?'

'Let's forget about it.'

'You brought it up.'

'I just wanted to be sure.'

'I don't know why you want to make such a mystery of it,' Jordan said. She lit another cigarette. He noticed that her hands were still unsteady. 'You smoke too much.'

'Only sometimes. Do you still want me to stop on here?'

'You haven't changed your mind, have you?'

'I was still making it up.'

'Is there anything I can do to help you decide to stay? I obviously can't guarantee to keep out of your dreams.'

'You won't get it out of me that way.'

Emboldened by her small smile, Jordan said, 'Well, at least tell me this much: did I seem to enjoy being in your dream?'

She got up. 'Shall I make another pot of tea or are you ready to go on to coffee?'

'Make which ever you prefer.'

'Say which you want.'

'I'll leave it to you.'

'You don't sulk, do you?' she asked. 'I can't abide people who sulk.'

'I don't sulk; I show my displeasure.'

'I wish I'd never mentioned it.'

'But you wanted to be sure.'

'There's no need for sarcasm, either.'

'Well, what did you want to be sure of, for heaven's sake?'

She banged down the full kettle, slipped home the plug, closed the switch.

'If you must know,' she said, 'I didn't want to spend the next couple of weeks wondering if I might be pregnant.'

'You mean to say,' Jordan said, on his feet now, 'that you think I'm the kind of man who'd creep into your bed and take advantage of you while you didn't know what you were doing?'

'What are you getting mad about?'

'I'm wondering what sort of a man you take me for.'

'You are a man, aren't you?'

'What does that mean?'

'If I *invited* you into my bed, what would you do?'

Jordan turned to the window. His neighbour's garden fire was burning well now. A sudden spring of breeze fanned out the smoke before lifting it over a nearby roof. He was astounded that things between them had come so far so fast. It was not the way he'd imagined it at all.

'Can't you answer?'

He tried to keep his voice cool and level. 'What makes you think I'm interested in you that way?'

'If you're not, you're not. But I want to know. I want to know if that's what you had in mind when you asked me to come and live here.' When he didn't speak, she went on, 'I reckon I've a right to know that much.'

'Which is the answer that will keep you here?' Jordan asked.

'Try telling the truth.'

Whatever happened now, Jordan thought, things could never be the same. He felt like a small boy caught in some shameful action. Yet if he denied what he wanted he was sure she would feel obliged to go.

'I want to make love to you,' he said.

She was silent for so long he thought she must have left the room. He forced himself round.

'Did you hear me?'

'I heard you.' She was pouring boiling water into the teapot. 'You should have said. You should have told me.'

He stepped towards her and put his hands on her shoulders from behind. 'Audrey . . .' But she turned and brushed past him to set the teapot down on the table.

'Don't be in such a rush,' she said. 'It's time I made your breakfast. And then there's one or two things we have to talk about.'

'I'm scared stiff of getting pregant,' she was saying to him a long time later that day.

'You won't.'

'You can get something, can't you?'

'Tomorrow.'

Reminded by his neighbour's activity, he had spent most of the daylight hours in his neglected garden, keeping away from her and trying through physical labour to curb his mounting excitement. But images of her came again and again to fill his mind until, by nightfall, he was almost sick with longing and could only toy with his evening meal.

'You should have said. You should have told me.'

'I didn't know how. I didn't want to frighten you off. I hoped you'd come to the idea in your own time.'

'I don't know what it is you see in me.'

'I'd like to look after you. Do things for you. Nice things.'

'What for? I'm not your sort.'

'Perhaps that's why.'

'You're a gentleman. I'm nothing.'

'You're talking rubbish.'

'You know next to nothing about me.'

'You're what you let yourself be.'

'Seems to me I've nearly always been forced.'

'I won't force you,' Jordan said.

'No, you'd kill me with kindness.'

'Would?'

'You will. If I let you.'

'Promise me,' she was saying to him now. 'Promise you won't go any further than I let you.'

'I promise.'

Her mouth moved against his as her tongue probed. She tasted faintly of tobacco smoke. He shuddered as her hand explored his groin. When his own hand slid down across her flat belly she took it firmly and led it to her breasts. He clutched them and gasped as the spasm started in him.

The papers were needed for the meeting. Mrs Perrins said she had searched high and low but could not find them. 'You took them home with you, didn't you? I remember you saying you'd take them home to read in peace.'

'I thought I'd brought them back.'

He was slipping. He forgot things. Yet he felt in bounding physical condition. She had noticed the difference in him and he had caught her once or twice looking at him in a mildly speculative way.

He had just returned to his office after lunch. The meeting was called for three-thirty.

'I shall have to go back and look for them,' he said. 'We can't manage without them, that's for sure.'

He left the car in the street and walked up the drive. The house was afternoon-still. Audrey got most of her work done in the morning. He supposed she could have gone out, though he knew she quite often took a nap after lunch.

He went straight upstairs, his feet moving lightly, two steps at a time. Her door stood ajar. It opened without a sound over the carpet as he stepped round. She was asleep, the sheet down to her hips exposing the long curve of her naked back. Jordan thought the man lying on the other side of her was sleeping too until, in the second before the closing door cut off his view, a head lifted off the pillow and Harry's eyes looked directly into his.

The telephone in the hall began to ring as he got to the top of the stairs. He was down and reaching for it when he heard movement on the landing and she came into view, drawing a wrap about her. She paused for a second as she saw him and he noticed that she could not resist a quick look behind her.

'What are you – ?'

There was something in her face beyond instinctive apprehension: something he couldn't in his present state define, and which was gone almost as soon as he had discerned it.

He waved her to silence, the receiver filled with the effusive apologies of his secretary. He listened, said a couple of words and hung up.

'How long have you been back?' Her voice was lifted, unusually carrying.

'I've just come in.'

'Is there something wrong?'

'I came to get some papers, but my secretary's found them.'

'I was lying down.'

'So I gathered.'

He felt suddenly as though he would fall. She took a step towards him as his hand groped for the wooden arm of the chair beside the telephone. He sat down heavily, bending forward to thrust his head between his knees.

'What's the matter? Aren't you well?'

'I'll be all right.'

'You look as pale as lard,' she said when he straightened up. Her hands fluttered at the stuff of the wrap, drawing it closer, smoothing it down.

'I just went dizzy for a second, that's all.'

'Shouldn't you rest for a while?'

She had to say that, he thought. She couldn't avoid saying that.

'I've got an important meeting. They can't hold it without me.' He got up and stood very still for a moment, checking his balance.

'Well, you just be careful driving.'

'I will.' He turned at the door. 'By the way, there's been a slight change in my plans.' Her eyes held his. He was the first to look away. 'I have to entertain a customer. I shan't be in for dinner.'

From his office Jordan drove into the city centre and found a place to park. He went into a pub and drank two large whiskies then walked across the street to a cinema. He sat in an almost empty auditorium until he became slowly aware that what he was looking at on the screen was what he had seen when he first came in. Then he went out into streets upon which night had fallen and drove home.

The house was in darkness. He went about the ground floor, switching on lights, before going upstairs to her room. The wardrobe and drawers were empty of her belongings. The suitcase she had brought them in was gone too.

Nearly two weeks passed before Jordan brought himself to drive across the city to Birtmore Street. Time after time he had conjured up the image of her as she had come down the stairs towards him, drawing the wrap around her nakedness. Again and again he had analysed and re-interpreted the expression on her face as she had seen him. Slowly, over the days and nights, the idea grew in him that her look had been that of one who realises she has committed perhaps the greatest folly of her life. Only when this notion became fixed in him did his misery relax its paralysing grip. Only then did some lingering vestige of hope tell him that, in spite of everything, all might not yet be lost.

When he had struck a match by the dark glass of the door and rung what he took to be her bell, he tried once more to rehearse what he might say, and once more gave up the attempt. He did not know what he would say until he saw her reaction. Perhaps he would need to say very little. He wanted her back. She would know that when she saw him.

He rang again, making a slow count to five as his finger held the push. More than likely she was at the pub, working. He had thought of looking in there first, but balked at the prospect of meeting her again for the first time in public. But better that than not seeing her at all. There was no need for a fuss. His appearing would tell her and if there was in her anything at all of what he had imagined – no, known – she would make it in her way to have a private word.

The voice challenged him as he reached the gate. 'Were you ringing my bell?' A girl stood in the now lighted doorway, a plump girl, as round as a bouncing ball. She took a couple of steps back into the hall as Jordan approached her. A deep lateral crease in her pale green T-shirt marked the division between belly and breasts. 'What d'you want?'

'I was hoping to see Mrs Nugent.'

'You were ringing *my* bell.'

'Sorry. I thought it was hers. Is she in, d'you know?'

'Who did you say?'

'Mrs Nugent.'

The girl's right hand had a firm hold on the edge of the door, as though she were ready to slam it on him.

'I don't know anybody of that name.'

Do I look like a woman-killer? Jordan thought. And yet, what did a woman-killer look like? He kept a reassuring distance as he said, 'She lives in the first floor back.'

'She doesn't, you know,' the girl said. 'That's where I live, as of yesterday. And I'd be out as of tomorrow, if I'd anywhere better to go. It's a right bloody dump.'

'She can only just have moved,' Jordan said helplessly. 'Are you sure you've not seen her?'

'What name was it again?'

'Nugent. Audrey Nugent. She was sometimes with a man

called Harry. In his middle thirties, well built, dark curly hair.'

'There's nobody like that here now, mister.'

'Then I'm sorry to have troubled you.'

'If you say so.' As the door began to close, she added, 'Better luck next time.'

Jordan forced himself to enter the Royal Oak. It was busier than before and he had to wait to catch the landlord's eye.

'You might remember me asking for Mrs Nugent some time back.'

'Oh, yes?'

'Does she still work here?'

'Hasn't for some while now. I heard she'd gone to house-keep for a feller, somewhere the other side of town.'

'You've no idea where I might find her now?'

'Did you find her before?'

'Yes.'

'You shouldn't have lost her again, then. Scotch, wasn't it?'

'No, thanks,' Jordan said. 'So you've no idea where she is?'

'None at all, mate.' The man was already moving away.

Jordan called at the Beehive and drank a couple of pints. He had done that two or three times while she was with him. She had sent him. 'Walk on to the Beehive and have a pint while I watch the telly. Do you good.' He had stood at the bar, savouring the cool beer and recalling in his mind's eye the first time he had seen her and the extraordinary warmth and charm of her smile; his own smile, bestowed like a blessing on all who came near him, wrapped round the knowledge of just where she was, what she was doing, who she was waiting for.

The beer got to him quickly. He stood with his head down in his shoulders, both hands on the bar counter, thinking again of how she had looked as she came downstairs, with upper-most in her mind, the instant after seeing him, the realisation of all she had put at risk. 'I would tell you,' he said softly, aloud, 'if I knew where you were.'

He went home. He hated the place now and wondered how quickly he could sell it. But suppose he did sell it and, as he had with her, she came looking for him and did not know where he had gone? How his wife would have mocked him . . .

On a thought, he went straight upstairs to his wife's room, where he opened the wardobes. The fur cape was gone, as was her jewellery box from the dressing-table drawer. He couldn't think now why it had not occurred to him to look before. Downstairs again, he crossed the hall to the small sitting-room that his wife had used in the evenings, a room he had no more than glanced into for several weeks. The display cabinet housing her father's collection of snuff-boxes stood against the wall behind the door. A sliver of glass broke under his feet. It had needed only a small hole, just big enough for an arm to reach in. The heel of a woman's shoe could easily have made that.

When, a few weeks later, the chairman of the group that controlled his firm called Jordan to head office to tell him personally that owing to a major reorganisation in difficult times the board was compelled to ask him to take early retirement, but there was a sizeable golden handshake and his pension to see him through in comfort (and, after all, wasn't business these days full of younger men who had every intention of throwing off their responsibilities when they were little older than Jordan was now?), Jordan sat as though he was not hearing a word that was said to him.

'How did he take it?' a fellow director asked afterwards.

'How did he take it?'

'Was he surprised, shocked, resentful?'

'It's hard to describe. I can't remember his saying a single word. He was like a man who's given up altogether, a man who quite simply doesn't give a damn about anything.'